Hook or Crook

Hook or Crook

Gerald Hammond

St. Martin's Press
New York

Library of Congress Cataloging-in-Publication Data

Hammond, Gerald
    Hook or crook / Gerald Hammond.
        p.   cm.
    ISBN 0-312-11825-2
    I. Title.
    PR6058.A55456H65   1995
    823'.914—dc20   94-24621
                                                        CIP

First published in Great Britain by Macmillan London Limited

First U.S. Edition: January 1995
10 9 8 7 6 5 4 3 2 1

ONE

'Shit!' Eric said loudly.

I knew only too well what that meant. He was into the reeds again. I waded ashore and carried my own rod upstream along the bank, standing it safely upright against the fence where the trees began. Eric had not only hooked the reeds at the river's edge but he had managed to tangle the thin nylon leader in and out and round about. I took to the water again and began to unravel the knitting. 'How in Mary's name did you manage this?' I asked him.

He produced the shy smile which sat so incongruously on the face of such a large man, among the jowls and padding. 'Just a knack,' he said.

It was quickest to break off and withdraw some of the reeds. 'I've told you before,' I said, trying not to sound irritable. 'That rod has too soft an action for you. By the time you get any power into the back-cast, most of your rod's gone past the vertical and you don't have a hope in hell of keeping the back-cast high. I don't care what sort of bargain you got, it was still money down the drain. You should have spoken to me first. I never try to sell you anything that won't suit you. Try again with my rod.'

He had waded to join me. He leaned back against the bank and lit a cigar. 'Hardly worth the bother,' he said. 'We don't seem to be doing any good here.'

He had a point. I had never seen the Spey so low. A breathless calm and a bright sun were adding to the difficulties. 'We could knock off if you like,' I suggested.

1

'Things sometimes improve towards evening.'

I looked up in time to see him shaking his head emphatically. 'If you think there's a hope in hell,' he said, 'I'm game to fish on. Couldn't we try spinning?'

'The Spey isn't a spinning river,' I said. I could have added that the tangle Eric could get into with monofilament line and a fixed-spool reel was beyond belief, but I spared his feelings. Besides, he already knew it.

Eric Bell was inexperienced but keen. Several years earlier, after a ten-year marriage, his much-loved wife had died while striving, unsuccessfully, to bear him a child. Heartbroken, he had been trying to recuperate at the home of a sister-in-law near Newton Lauder and, I suspected, had unsettled her family with his constant moping. In desperation, the lady had decided that he needed another outlet for his emotions and suggested a visit to our shop. She took the precaution of phoning Keith, my partner, begging him to get Eric interested in something, anything, before he drove her mad.

Keith owed the lady's husband a favour. And he is never averse to selling a gun. He introduced Eric to the various disciplines of clay-pigeon shooting and also took him out in pursuit of rabbit and woodpigeon.

Eric had taken to the sport but, Keith told me, he would never be more than a moderate shot and, moreover, until Eric got over his bereavement and began to concentrate, he would never measure up to Keith's exacting standard of safe behaviour. When Eric expressed a mild interest in fishing, Keith had handed him over to me with a sigh of relief.

As a salmon fisherman, Eric had as little talent as he had for shooting. But he had the two most important qualifications: dedication and money. He was, I gathered, the proprietor of a string of up-market garment shops spread through the south of England. (He was the only man I ever knew who could discuss the finer points of ladies' underwear without sounding either embarrassed or salacious.) With no other calls on his considerable income he could afford to indulge his new-found hobbies.

I had taught him to cast to the best of his ham-fisted ability and, by standing at his elbow and directing his every movement, I had put him into his first couple of salmon. Since then, he had made visits to Norway and Canada in search of ever better sport but, lacking a patient mentor, had been disappointed. So he had returned to the fold and was quite happy to pay my fees as an instructor in order to have me act as his ghillie.

A sudden phone-call earlier in the summer had announced that Eric was thinking of taking a beat on the Spey for a fortnight. Would I, he asked, care to come with him? I consulted quickly. Keith said 'Go'. Janet, my wife, who had been waiting for a chance to invite a widowed schoolfriend with two children to visit our tiny flat, also said 'Go'. Keith, I knew, only wanted me out of the way so that he could relegate the rods and waders to the back of the shop and give prominence to guns and shooting gear, but I went anyway. Speyside is not only famous for malt whisky. I have never objected to being well paid to go fishing in a top salmon river set in beautiful countryside, nor to being wined and dined by a host as lavish as Eric.

I finished detaching his line from the reeds. 'Your fly's looking distinctly secondhand,' I said. 'Try my rod while I put on another.'

'Maybe a larger fly would do the trick,' he said.

'Definitely not,' I told him. He took my rod, waded out and began to false cast to get out some line. I had to duck once to avoid being hooked. 'You're on the Spey,' I said. 'Try Spey casting. I've shown you how often enough.' At least with a Spey cast his fly need never come behind him.

'It never works for me,' he said.

'Then do a simple roll cast. Try to get right under the far bank.'

Thanks to an accident some years before I am short of three fingers on my right hand. I would have allowed Eric to tie on his own fly except that his efforts in that direction usually turned the fly into something resembling a spider in its web. I finished pulling the tucked blood-knot up tight at last. Eric had plenty of line out but his first attempt at a roll cast with my rod laid a pattern on the water that reminded me of a child's scribble.

'Don't make such heavy weather of it,' I said. 'Be gentle. Pretend that you're the fairy queen, waving a magic wand.'

He grinned at me and said, 'Abracadabra.' The rod tip made a gentle circle in the air and the same circle rolled beautifully along, laying the line straight across the river, angling downstream. The fly landed gently under the far bank. 'Good Lord!' Eric said.

'Power's never a substitute for doing it right,' I said. 'Mend your line.' He flicked the rod to put a curve into the floating line. 'Upstream, you prat,' I said.

'Sorry, Wal.' He flicked the other way.

With an upstream belly in the line, the less sluggish midstream current would not be dragging unnaturally at the fly, which would now be fishing gently along the lies under the bank.

I watched anxiously. Eric was my protégé and my host. For once he had done his part correctly, but success depended on the co-operation of salmon which had so far proved either uncooperative or absent.

The fly, moving now too fast, began to swing round the tail of the pool where a glide, smooth as glass, led to the brink of a low fall. Salmon sometimes lie just above such a fall, but I doubted whether Eric could cope with a take in such a position. The fly passed the glide and the swing of the line slowed.

'Come a few paces back towards the bank,' I said. 'Bring the rod slowly round until it's pointing towards me ... Now, start hand-lining in, a foot or two at a time, not too fast ...

The fly was moving up in a series of fish-like spurts below the nearer bank. Suddenly it stopped. I saw the

4

loose line between the reel and the bottom ring slide through Eric's fingers. He looked at me in a daze.

'Pull,' I said urgently, 'and then slack off immediately.'

He came to, gave a good pull and then let some line run free. After a pause, he said, 'What do you reckon, Wal?'

'You've got a salmon on.'

'I can't feel anything.'

It was hardly the time for a lesson. On the other hand, if he understood what was going on he might for once do it right. 'If you'd kept hauling at him, he'd have fought against you and gone down the leap and broken you. Give him a little line and he'll either settle down or move upstream against the pull of the slack line in the water. Look, he's moving now.' The floating line was coming round in a curve. 'Let him go up past you, then start to reel in. Keep the rod up.'

I was already on the bank. I hurried downstream and waded out. If Eric got it wrong and the salmon came down again, I might be able to head him away from the rapids.

When he felt the pull of the rod, the salmon began to fight. Eric followed, stumbling over the rocks in the river-bed. I shouted at him again to keep the rod up. They were going upstream so I followed along the bank. I think that I was shouting out more advice and encouragement which were probably contradictory and may have hindered more than they helped. Once Eric tripped and fell to his knees, but when he heaved himself to his feet the fish was still on.

In ten minutes, they were both exhausted. 'Come in to the bank,' I told Eric. 'Draw him into the shallows. Quick, before he gets his breath back.' But when he saw the loom of the human figures the fish was off again in one blaze of energy. There was a boulder in midstream and if he got the line around that he would break free. Eric gaped at me. 'Turn his head,' I gasped. 'Pull. Keep the line taut.' Eric pulled. The spring of the rod absorbed the shocks of the fighting fish but as long as his head was turned away from the big boulder his struggles only helped Eric to bring him towards the bank.

The tailer was already screwed into my wading staff. I slipped it over the fish's tail – a cock fish, faintly coloured and beginning to develop a kype or jaw-hook.

'Is it still takeable?' Eric asked anxiously. He was panting for breath, thoroughly wet but grinning all over his large face.

'He'd smoke very nicely,' I said. 'Do you want to keep him?'

'Are you mad? That fish has cost me a fortune. Of course I want to keep him.'

I administered a rap on the head with the priest and we lifted the salmon onto the bank and weighed him on my spring balance at a shade over ten pounds. Eric lay on his back and raised his legs, discharging several gallons of water from his thigh waders. Then nothing would do but for Eric to walk squelching to the car to fetch his camera and hold up the fish while I photographed them both from every possible angle.

When the fish was wrapped in damp grass and moss and safely bestowed in the shade, Eric found and lit a dry cigar.

'I like your rod,' he said.

'When we get back to the shop, I'll pick you out one exactly like it. Speak to me, next time, before you splash out good money on gear.'

'Maybe. I'd rather have that particular rod, if you'll sell it. It seems to be lucky for me.' He paused, frowning. 'Something's coming back to me. Something I glimpsed on the way past. In all the flurry and excitement it didn't register. But now, shouldn't we do something about . . . him?'

'Who's him?' I asked.

'Did I imagine him in the heat of the moment? Was he something thrown up by my fevered subconscious, thawed by the heat of the moment?' Eric led the way back towards where we had landed the salmon. 'No, I thought I wasn't dreaming.' He pointed.

In the shallows, only a few yards from where we had beached the salmon, a man's body lay face down in the water. Thinking back, I realized that I must have stepped over him, but my concentration had been totally on the fish while the body, which was dressed in muted colours and largely submerged, could have passed for a patch of weed in my peripheral vision. He was dark haired and wore chest waders and a green shirt. I stooped and touched his neck. He was as cold as the water. There could be no doubt that he was dead.

'Who do we call?' Eric asked me. 'Ambulance?'

'We call the police,' I told him. 'You'd better go and find a phone. It's your car and you saw him first.'

'If I must.' Eric grudged leaving the water now that his luck seemed to be on the turn, but he accepted my argument. He gathered up his fish in his arms like a baby and set off back to the car again.

I tried to settle down to a respectful vigil. But there was no movement within sight or sound except for the sluggish river. I soon felt an unease which I tried to dismiss as mere boredom. But my previous acquaintance with death had been limited to viewing the remains of an occasional relative in the seemly surroundings of a satin-lined casket, at which times I had been accompanied by other mourners. Those deaths had therefore been official and certified. However obviously defunct the man at my feet might be, nobody had told me that he was dead. The slow passing of the water over his shirt produced a faint movement which could be mistaken for breathing and a heartbeat . . .

An atavistic fear of the living dead is one of our deepest instincts. I backed away until those small movements were lost in distance. And if he should suddenly raise his head and come crawling out of the water, I would have a good head start.

Ten minutes passed without the least sign of a twitch.

7

The body became a mere inanimate object, too still to hold my attention. But beneath the surface of the river, life should be moving in the form of fish.

The man was well wedged among the stones. He was not going anywhere. On the other hand, I did not get many chances to fish the Spey without distractions. Eric was a lavish host and a good companion, but nursemaiding him was not conducive to catching fish. The man had himself been a fisherman. He would understand, I told myself.

Eric had lost his first cigar during his tussle with the fish, and salmon hate the taint of tobacco, so I moved upstream to a pool that we had covered earlier and began the endless business of cast and retrieve. A salmon parr grabbed the hook. I held the hook steady and let the little fish wriggle off. I had one half-hearted pull but no other takes. Soon I was lost in the mild trance that overtakes the angler on fishless days. My mind was somewhere below the surface of the water, trying to sense the whereabouts of the fish.

Some time later, the sound of approaching voices reminded me of the more serious business of life and death. I climbed the bank and hurried back to where the body was patiently waiting for attention and by the time two figures approached along the bank I was, I hoped, the very picture of a dutiful sentinel standing vigil over the sad remains.

'This is Wallace James,' Eric said. He had changed into dry clothes and left his thigh waders behind. He was carrying his huge chest waders in one hand and over his shoulder.

An average policeman would have given me a look that threw doubt on whether the name was real, whether anybody cared and what I was up to. The uniformed constable surprised me by first shaking my hand and then saying, 'We've met before. I attended one of your fishing courses, several years ago. I still read your articles.'

The young constable was a tall lad although Eric

dwarfed him. He had an open, friendly face, sandy hair and freckles. There was something in the voice with its soft, Highland inflections that touched my memory but I had no recollection of having seen him before until it dawned on me that, not many years earlier, he would have been smaller and still a schoolboy. A mental picture came to me of a boy blessed with great enthusiasm and insatiable curiosity who had been casting to perfection within twenty minutes of picking up a rod for the first time. Then I remembered him and felt at ease at once.

'McIver,' I said. 'Tony McIver. A pike took your biggest trout off the hook. You accepted the disaster philosophically, I remember. Are you still fishing?'

He looked gratified. 'When I can,' he said. His voice was deeper but otherwise just as I remembered it, with a gentle Highland lilt. 'I'm based just up the road. They don't let me at the salmon very often but there's trout in the tributaries and I fish for sea-trout now and again. It's been a terrible year, though. Just terrible! Catches are down by half.'

'No doubt of it. Mr Bell told you that we've found a body?'

He looked put out. To the true Highlander, to whom social contact may be a rare and precious commodity, business must always be preceded by courteous discussion of the topics of the day. And bodies, I knew, were of much less pressing interest than the fishing. A body will remain a body but the state of the fishing, on which prosperity or even survival may depend, can change in a moment.

Constable McIver decided to make allowances. 'He did. So we had better take a look at it.'

We led him to the river's brink and he stood looking at the scene for a minute.

'You took long enough,' I told Eric.

'I went back to the hotel for a change of clothes.'

'You went back to the hotel to get your fish into the hotel freezer,' I said.

9

Eric shrugged and looked sly.

PC McIver was not dressed for wading. Eric climbed into his tent-like waders and we drew the body clear of the water. McIver rolled it over gently. 'Do you recognize him?' he asked.

The man had been of about my height, which is no more than average, but beefier. It was difficult to guess his age. I put him at fifty or perhaps a little over, although the wrinkling produced by a prolonged immersion made him look much older. He still had a full head of hair without any grey in it and I guessed that he had had recourse to one of the new generation of hair-dyes. He had a firm jaw and prominent eyebrow ridges, but in death his expression was one of polite surprise.

Eric shook his head. 'Never seen him before,' I said.

'Then he is not, for instance, the tenant of the beat opposite?'

'We've never seen anybody fishing from the other bank,' I said.

'Is that so?' McIver said quickly. I wondered what significance he found in my statement until I realized that he had recognized a chance to scrounge some free fishing.

He returned his attention to the body and suddenly stooped to point at the corpse's cheek. I have a profound distaste for human bodies (although dead members of the animal kingdom bother me not at all) and I had been trying to avoid looking at what had once been another man, but involuntarily I followed the finger which was pointing at what, in my first fleeting glance, I had taken to be a leaf or a scrap of water-weed. The same glance took in an unpleasant dent in the corpse's brow, made worse rather than better by the lack of blood or bruising. The flesh, where it had opened, looked bleached. I averted my eyes again, quickly.

'A salmon fly, hooked into his cheek,' Eric said. 'Stoat's tail, is it?'

'Stoat and silver,' said the constable. 'Number Five hook, would you say?'

10

'Four,' I said, without looking again. Keith Calder, my partner, would by now have been down on his knees, examining the body and getting in the way of the police, but I have never had his appetite for a mystery.

Eric was becoming interested, even if he was finding the mystery itself a disappointment. 'Seems to me,' he said, 'the man made a bad cast and hooked himself. Between pain and surprise, he fell and hit his head.'

'Snapping his leader at the same time?' McIver enquired. 'I think the hook would have pulled through the skin before the leader would have broken. Well now, this is too heavy for me. I'll radio for help.'

'We could have our lunch,' Eric suggested. 'And then ... Would there be any objection if we went on fishing?'

McIver hesitated, his hand hovering over the radio on his lapel. Eventually the instincts of the angler triumphed over those of the policeman. 'You've paid enough for the fishing,' he said. 'It seems a pity to let it go to waste. Go downstream, though, for the moment. Anything that happened to the mannie happened above here.'

TWO

I walked upstream to fetch our lunches from Eric's car, which was parked on the narrow grass verge beside the first bridge.

When Eric had first visited the shop he had already been big, six foot six at least and broad in proportion, but there had been little flesh on his bones. During the years of widowerhood, in addition to fishing and shooting, he had, in common with many who are nursing an inner wound, taken to eating as a hobby and almost an art-form. He now topped three hundred pounds and tried cars on as if they had been shoes. The most comfortable fit that he had found in keeping with his new image as a fieldsportsman was a large, Japanese four-wheel-drive monster. The small police panda car parked nose to nose with it looked like a toy.

I fetched our lunch basket out of the back, but before setting off I rested it on the parapet for a minute looking thoughtfully down at the water. Shadows on the bottom led my eye to several beautifully camouflaged trout; and through my Polaroid sunglasses I could make out a salmon resting in the shadow of a rock, but it would not be in a taking mood nor was my mind on fishing for the moment. The basket was heavy and I arrived back sweating in the sunshine.

PC McIver was standing guard by the body. I gave him a sandwich and a can of beer as I passed by, which was as much as he could be persuaded to accept; and I found Eric two pools lower down, wading in the shallows and casting with my rod. He joined me on the bank. No trees had been allowed to grow close to the water, but twenty yards back we were able to settle ourselves on a hummock in the shade of a silver birch.

Eric was prepared to work his way through a stack of sandwiches, several pies and a salad with enough chicken legs to have kept a whole flock on foot, followed by a slab of cake and cheese and biscuits, the whole washed down with a bottle of claret. My appetite was more quickly satisfied by a couple of pâté sandwiches, a very small paper cup of the wine and a mug of coffee.

I took up my rod and wandered back to the water. The prospects for salmon remained poor, but salmon fishing always retains an element of chuck-it-and-chance-it and I enjoy the more precise challenge of trout fishing. Several fish were rising to the insect life hatching on the water.

I dipped into my bag and tied on a team of three flies on a finer cast. I dislike leaving expensive rods locked in a car, so my trout rod was back at the hotel. A fifteen-foot salmon rod was a clumsy tool for short and accurate upstream casting, but at least it enabled me to keep back from the river's edge and out of the sight of the fish.

By the time that Eric came at last to join me, I had landed two trout of almost a pound each and had hooked another. But my third fish had managed to snag me on something. I put down the rod and waded into the shallows. The trout had gobbled my point fly. I knocked it on the head, used the disgorger to detach it and tossed it to join its fellows on the bank.

'They're just tiddlers,' Eric said.

'But I got them,' I pointed out. 'Give me another hour and I'll match the weight of your salmon. And at least they're there. You probably caught the only takeable salmon on the beat.'

He flashed a sudden grin at me. Gone were the dull and uneven teeth of previous years. As he explained it, a pretty young dentist had said, 'Let me take all this away from you,' and the result was a smile that was almost

13

blinding in the sunshine. 'All right,' he said. 'Let's have a go at the brownies.'

'Hang on a minute,' I told him while I groped under the water. My top dropper had hooked into something soft which moved in the water. For a moment I thought that I had found another body and my stomach gave a preparatory heave. But the object was a fishing bag. I lifted it towards the bank. Water poured out, bringing with it a host of small fish, mostly salmon fry. I decanted them carefully into the river, leaving in the bag a bulky object which turned out to be another salmon of, I guessed, about twelve pounds. It was much nibbled, but it had once been a good, fresh-run fish.

Eric was towering over me. 'There you are,' he said. 'There are more salmon to be had in the river.'

'Maybe. The police should see this. Do you want to resume fishing?'

'And miss all the fun? No, I'm coming with you.'

'If that's your idea of fun, you'll enjoy carrying the food basket,' I told him. 'It may as well go back to the car.'

Eric picked up the basket, which was much lighter than before, after placing his shoes on top. I gathered up our rods and trappings. At the tail of the next pool we met PC McIver. 'I was coming to look for you,' he said. 'They want to ask you some questions.'

I nodded. I had been awaiting the summons in some trepidation. I hate talking with strangers outside my own territory. This may stem from the stammer that had made my youth a misery and still plagues me slightly when I get nervous, although perhaps I am confusing cause and effect. Whatever the reason, I dislike confrontations unless I am in control.

I handed over the sodden fishing bag to McIver. 'I've just found this,' I told him. He looked inside and his eyebrows shot up but he made no comment.

The body seemed to be where we had last seen it. It was now at the centre of a hive of activity. I saw the flash of a bulb. On the outskirts of the group, two men in uniform were waiting with a stretcher.

McIver left us at the edge of the trees, well back from the scene, while he approached the throng. There was some discussion and headshaking over the fishing bag and its contents. McIver returned with two men in plain clothes.

'This is Mr James, sir. Wallace James. And Mr Eric Bell. They found the body and the bag. DCI Fergusson,' he told us. Fergusson was a bull of a man, although he looked small beside Eric. There was a stuborn look to his face and I thought that his small eyes were looking for a reason to become suspicious.

I glanced at the other man, who was cast in the lean, dark, Celtic mould. 'And DS Lennox,' McIver added.

The detective sergeant produced what at first I took for a small radio and switched it on. 'You don't mind if we tape our discussion,' he told me. The tone of his voice suggested that it was not a question. 'It saves a whole skelp of note-taking.'

'And,' said Eric, 'without being any more open to accusations of falsification.'

DCI Fergusson frowned loftily. McIver looked shocked. I probably looked astonished. It was unlike the placid Eric to come up with such a double-edged comment. Lennox only smiled and said, 'Very much less. You have had problems of that kind?'

'Never,' Eric said. 'A friend of mine . . . '

'That would be in London, no doubt,' said Lennox quellingly.

'Mr James,' the DCI said, but to the tape recorder rather than to me, 'it seems a strange coincidence that the man who found the body also found what may be the dead man's bag.'

Immediately, remembering that the finder of a body ranks high among the suspects, I felt guilty and was sure that I looked it. Eric decided to answer for me. 'In the first place,' he said, 'Mr James didn't find the body. I saw it first. In the second place, he was fishing with a team of three flies and he caught several trout.' (I opened my own bag and exhibited my catch. The DCI seemed unimpressed but Lennox and Tony McIver leaned over for a closer look.) 'When each of those fish was hooked it would dash to and fro and the two spare hooks would dance all over the place. If the bag had come to rest anywhere within casting range, it would have been a stranger coincidence if he had failed to hook it.'

DCI Fergusson looked at Eric suspiciously. Eric, out of the depths of his ignorance, was only stating the apparently obvious, but his vast bulk gave him an air of authority which suggested that he might know what he was talking about.

'That is probably so,' Lennox said.

'Very well,' Fergusson said at last. He turned slightly, putting Eric behind his right shoulder and out of his own view. 'Mr James, Constable McIver tells me that you are a well-known fisherman. Is that correct?'

Questions of that sort make me want to fall over my feet. 'I'm well known to my wife and a few friends,' I said. 'Beyond that . . . '

'But you're a qualified instructor? And you write articles in the fishing magazines?'

'Well, yes,' I said.

He hesitated for some seconds before deciding to open up. 'On the face of it, this looks like a common accident. But PC McIver says that he has doubts. Has he discussed his reasoning with you?'

'Not a word,' I said.

'Please let me have your opinion.' He did not say that he would value or appreciate it, nor that he would even consider it, just please to give it.

My doubts about the putative accident were still tentative. I decided to apply the only available test before exposing them to ridicule. 'If he had a fly-box on him, I'd like to see inside it.'

Fergusson took the tape recorder from the Detective Sergeant and nodded. The DS hurried off. 'Why do you want to see his . . . ' Fergusson boggled at saying 'flies'. ' . . . fly-box?' he finished after a pause.

'There are too many unknowns. One of them is, was he a competent fisherman?'

16

'What difference would that make?'

'I'll have to go back to basics—'

Lennox returned, bringing with him a man in a plastic overall and plastic gloves who opened and displayed a flat fly-box under my nose without allowing me to touch it. 'It was in the pocket at the top of his waders,' Lennox said.

Two rows of salmon flies were hooked neatly into the foam backing, ranging from large to small, bright on one side and dark on the other. I nodded and the man closed the box and carried it off.

'Well?' Fergusson demanded.

'I can only make assumptions,' I said weakly.

'Of course, at this stage. That's what I want.'

'Very well. I think there's more to this than meets the eye. It may turn out to be a simple accident, but not that damn simple.'

Fergusson pushed his square jaw out at me. 'You could tell all that by looking in his box?'

'No,' I said.

He sighed. 'All right. Go back to basics.'

Eric, seeing that I was about to hold forth, looked set to take a seat on the lunch basket, property of the hotel. Rather than have him flatten it, I sat down there myself, allowing the others to tower over me. Eric moved sideways to where he could rest his back against a tree.

'Usually,' I said, 'there isn't a day in the year that a salmon isn't coming up the Spey. But this has been an upside-down year. The Spey gets its water from the snow melting on the Grampian, Monadhliath, Badenoch and Cairngorm mountains. But last winter was exceptionally mild. There was little snow to melt up there and the summer's been very dry. The river's about as low as it can possibly get. Very few fish are being taken and none of those is fresh run. Yet, if that was the dead man's bag, he had a fresh-run fish in it. It's looking a bit tatty now and trout and salmon fry have been nibbling at it, but there's no doubt about it.'

Fergusson glanced at Lennox, who nodded.

I was speaking with more confidence. Words came more

easily now that I was on my own subject. 'I wanted to look in his fly-box to see whether the man was a competent fisherman. And he was. A beginner tends to fill his box with weird and wonderful flies in the hope that one of them will compensate as if by magic for his lack of skill. That box held a sensible range of flies for all conditions. But it told me quite a lot more.'

Fergusson's eyes were beginning to glaze. 'Like what?' he said.

'Those flies weren't bought out of a shop. They were hand tied, and all by the same hand which suggests that he tied them himself. And that was his own fly stuck in his cheek. The dressing was a match and there was a corresponding gap in his box.'

'Ah,' Fergusson said wisely.

'But,' I said, 'it wasn't a fly that a skilled fisherman would be using in these conditions. Much too large.' I saw that Fergusson was looking at the flies on my cast, which was hooked to the reel and wound tight. 'Nor those,' I said. 'Those are trout flies.' I opened my own fly-box. 'This is what I was using this morning.'

The Chief Inspector looked at my Garry Dog. 'But it's yellow,' he said, as though he had caught me out in a lie.

'There's a saying – bright day, bright fly,' I told him (the Chief Inspector looked up at the sky) 'but that's not my reason. I don't believe that salmon can distinguish the colour or tone of a fly being fished near the surface. I like a bright fly because sometimes I can see it in the water and be sure what it's doing. The salmon judges by size and movement. To it, the fly represents a small fish or a krill. The speed of the fly through the water has to be proportionate to the size of what it represents. It's not easy to fish the fly quickly in slow water and it's damn near impossible to fish it slowly in fast water. So you use a small fly when the water's sluggish and a bigger one when it's fast.'

The Chief Inspector looked round at the Spey. For most of its width, the trees on the far bank were reflected in its shining water. 'I thought the fly was supposed to represent

18

whatever food they were feeding on at the time.'

'For trout, yes. Salmon can't feed in fresh water. They're just snapping at anything irritating that gets in their way.'

He returned his eyes to my Garry Dog. 'The fly hooked in the dead man's cheek was twice the size of that one,' he said.

'Exactly. But in his fly-box he had bright and dark flies in a range of sizes. So he subscribed to the "bright day, bright fly" custom. Here, and in this weather, he'd have been using a smaller, brighter fly. And even if he'd managed to get a fish, it would be very unlikely to be fresh run.'

'So,' said the Chief Inspector. He paused again. 'What are you suggesting?'

'I don't know that I'm suggesting anything,' I said. 'I'm just pointing out anomalies. As, for instance, where's his rod?'

'On the bottom of the river?'

'Most rods have a cork handle. Even if the rest of the rod sinks, the handle usually floats up. And I was wondering . . . '

'Yes?'

'How did he manage to hook himself in the cheek in an upward direction?'

McIver opened his mouth but Fergusson, who evidently believed that constables should be seen and not heard, at least until spoken to, got in first. 'That was the point young McIver made. He said that hooks catch in clothing or in protuberances like lips or ears but that they rarely dig into a more or less flat surface.'

'I wouldn't go along with that all the way,' I said. 'I've had to dig a few hooks out of my pupils from time to time. I've known one or two hook their own cheeks if they've mistimed the cast. But your customer had two hooks of a treble in him and they'd gone in in an upward direction. The only man I ever saw manage a trick like that had handed his rod to somebody else, turned away and walked his head into the leader – that's the thin nylon

19

between the hook and the fishing line proper. The leader hooked over his ear or his spectacles, we never worked out which, so that the hook came upward into his cheek.'

The chief inspector's pause for thought was the longest yet. He hummed to himself while he deliberated. 'Right,' he said at last. 'What conclusions do you draw from all this?'

'None,' I said. 'That's your business. And I could dream up a passable explanation for everything we've said.'

'But taking everything together ... ?'

I shook my head.

The Chief Inspector turned on his heel as though to stamp off. I decided that Eric's first remark had made him hostile and unreceptive. But to my surprise he turned back. 'Listen,' he said. 'I'm not an idiot. I know that the dead man could, against the odds, have landed a fresh-run fish. He might have been trying a larger fly for some reason of his own. He might have stood his rod against a tree and walked into the leader just the way you said. After hooking himself, he might have stumbled into the water and hit his head on a rock. Yes?'

'He might,' I said.

'That combination of factors is possible. If we think that he might have got hooked during a quarrel and a fight and have been hit over the head a moment later, it makes just as much sense and rather less demand on coincidence. Now take it a stage further. Assume that he'd landed a fish, then got into a fight during which he hooked himself in the cheek, then was hit and, accidentally or deliberately, killed. Or else he was killed and somebody else reeled in his line and hooked him. Assume that those events took place somewhere else. Assume that somebody then moved the body here in order to disassociate the death from himself. That demands no coincidence at all. Right?'

I shrugged.

'Aye,' the Chief Inspector said irritably. 'You're not going to do my reasoning for me. And you're right. But that's the way your own mind was working. Be honest, now.'

20

'True,' I said. 'It sounds unlikely but it's the explanation that best fits the facts.'

'Well now. Maybe we're both being a little too fanciful. But if not, if he was moved, where would you say he was moved from?'

The Chief Inspector had come round from treating us as suspicious characters to making a reasonable request for help. I could hardly refuse. 'There should be enough water in his lungs for your forensic scientists to make a good guess,' I said.

'In about a fortnight's time. Science moves at its own pace.'

'Well, I can't speak for every river. But from here north has been very dry. On the other hand the Cairngorms, where the Aberdeenshire Dee rises, had heavy rain within the last week or two. I hear that the Dee's full of fish. Deeside isn't so far from here, going by Tomintoul.'

The Chief Inspector let out a deep breath. 'It was like pulling teeth,' he said, 'but at last I've got it out of you. If we don't get somewhere quickly I'll have to ask Grampian Police for help. Give the Sergeant your details, home addresses and where you're putting up and there'll be statements for you to sign in due course.'

'One moment,' I said.

He had again been on the point of turning away but he checked. 'Yes?'

'Did he have car keys on him?'

'I believe so.' Fergusson looked at Lennox who nodded.

'It's a long shot,' I said, 'but I may be able to help a bit more – assuming that I've helped at all and not sent you on a wild-goose chase. Coming here this morning, I noticed a vehicle tucked away behind some bushes. If I could borrow PC McIver and the keys, we could check it out.'

Fergusson nodded. 'You're not to interfere with any-thing,' he told McIver. 'Just see if they fit.' And to Lennox, 'Give McIver the keys.'

He walked off without another word, followed by Lennox.

THREE

As we trudged back towards the bridge I could see that, up on the road, several more cars and an ambulance were now parked along the verge. Young McIver had been playing the part of the calm, dispassionate police officer for the benefit of his superiors but he allowed himself to relax, bouncing ahead with puppyish enthusiasm. An inquiry into a sudden death, we gathered, was a welcome change from more humdrum duties.

'That's a relief,' he said over his shoulder. 'You might not have agreed with me. Not that I wanted there to have been any foul play, you understand, but . . . '

'You'd stuck your neck out?' I suggested.

'That is just about it.' We climbed the embankment to the car and stowed our rods in the outside rod-holders. 'And when the neck of a humble PC is stuck well out, DCI Fergusson is just the man to administer the chop.'

'We could both turn out to be wrong,' I said.

'Then he'll have his knife into me for ever after. He's a tough nut is Mr Fergusson.'

I kicked off my thigh waders and put on shoes. Eric was preparing to struggle out of his chest waders. 'Keep them on for another minute or two,' I told him.

Eric waited while I tied my laces. 'Quite right,' he said after a moment. 'Never explain.'

'I'm going to explain. Come onto the bridge.' We walked the few yards and leaned on the sun-warmed parapet, facing downstream. 'If he was brought from somewhere else – and it's still a big if – he was probably dropped from here. After all, it's the nearest point to which you could bring a vehicle, upstream of where we found him. I can't see anyone carrying a body along the bank, where the water bailiff might be lurking, when they could stop the car and roll him over.'

'The whole area will be searched, as a matter of routine,' McIver said.

'Let's consider a short cut. Where's his rod? It would make no sense to drop him in here and leave his rod somewhere else. And if it had been carried down by what little current there is, it would have caught up in the rocks before going any further down than we've fished. We'd have seen the handle. But take a look down at the weed.' The river-bed was clean and stony under the clear water, but downstream of each of the two supporting piers was a triangle of thick water-weed. 'If a rod was dropped butt-first and it landed in the weed, it might easily stay caught up underwater.'

We peered down hopefully. Small parr were darting in and out of the weed.

'I think I see something,' Eric said. 'It's in the shadow, but there seems to be a thin line sticking out of the weed. We could fish for it from here.'

'Easier waded for,' I said. 'With the water as low as this, you could wade out and take a look at it. If that's in order?'

'I don't see why not,' McIver said slowly. 'You would not be spoiling any evidence, underwater on bare stones. Go ahead.'

While Eric took the well-worn path down from the bridge and waded cautiously into the deeper water cut by the flow through the arches, McIver looked down into the grass that had sprouted between the tarmac and the stone of the parapet. 'Don't touch,' he said suddenly, 'but look at this.'

'This' was a fisherman's folding knife, complete with scissors and descaler. 'I wondered why he did not have such a thing in his pocket,' McIver added.

Eric was making plaintive noises down below. We looked down into his moon-face. 'It's a rod all right,' he said. 'Carbon fibre, about a twelve-footer. Shall I bring it up?'

'If it's secure there, leave it,' said McIver. 'Keep an eye on our finds while I go and tell the Chief Inspector.'

He hurried back the way we had come. Eric climbed up to the roadway. I showed him the knife.

'Could be anybody's,' Eric said. 'And it's stainless steel, it wouldn't rust. It could have been there for weeks. But it begins to add together. A knife's easily dropped, but you'd miss it and go back. But if it fell out of a dead man's bag or the pocket of his chest waders . . . '

'And that's as much as anyone can say for the moment.'

I finished the coffee and Eric had a can of beer while we waited. Constable McIver returned at last. 'They're just coming,' he said. 'We can go and look at the car.'

'It wasn't a car,' I said. 'I think it was either a van or one of those campers, a motor-caravan.'

'Not a proper caravan for towing?'

'I doubt it. The roof was the wrong shape. It was at least half a mile away. We'd better drive.'

Eric began to struggle out of his waders again, while looking with disfavour at the small panda car. 'I could wear that thing for a roller-skate,' he said. 'We'll take mine.'

'You can stay and stand guard,' I suggested. We had an understanding that once the wine had begun to flow I would do the driving, but I had no desire to turn his monster in a narrow road which was becoming as cluttered as a municipal car-park.

'You're not leaving me out in the cold, so don't try,' Eric said. He heaved himself into his own passenger seat. 'Anyway, stand guard over what? Here they come.'

The Chief Inspector and another man were approaching along the river bank. I climbed resignedly into Eric's driving seat, which had begun to settle under his considerable weight, and started the engine. There was room for three in the front, but not if one of the three was Eric.

24

McIver got up into the rear. The interior was uncomfortably hot after a morning in the sun.

I drove on, reversed carefully into the mouth of a farm-road and came back. The Chief Inspector was already crouched over the knife in the grass. I slowed, ready to stop beside him, but he straightened up, more to get his backside out of the way than for any other reason, and waved us on. 'Don't take long over it,' he called to McIver as we went by. 'Touch nothing. Look and report.'

'Yes, sir,' McIver said. 'Three bags full,' he added as soon as we were clear.

Now that I was driving, I had less attention to spare for the few landmarks that I had noticed earlier. I had a vague recollection of bushes in the foreground and tall trees further back, all near a slight bend in the road. I rather thought that the open fields on the other side had held cattle. At the second such place that we came to, I spotted the roof of a vehicle and turned into a broad but rough track which zigged and then zagged, widened where heavy traffic had been manoeuvring and then disappeared in the direction of the trees. A stack of logs suggested that foresters had been at work.

The motor-caravan was parked at a tilt on the uneven ground. I pulled up some yards away and McIver got down. He walked with care, watching his feet, although the ground was baked too hard to show any recent tracks. I followed him and Eric came lumbering along behind.

'Look but don't touch,' McIver said, paraphrasing his superior.

'You sound like a girl I used to know,' Eric grumbled. 'I'll tell you one thing. He never slept here. Look at the slope. He'd have rolled out of the bunk.'

The curtains were drawn back and the interior looked very tidy. A tube with a lockable cap on the end was bolted to the roof, presumably for the safe storage of fishing rods. McIver unlocked the driver's door and quickly locked it again. 'The key fits,' he said. 'That's all we came to find out. Back we go.'

We set off back. At least one more car had arrived but

I managed to park Eric's vehicle where other traffic would be able to squeeze by.

Two men were now picking with great care through the fringe of grass, collecting ring-pulls and chocolate wrappings, while the Chief Inspector stared glumly down into the water. McIver hurried to report. We followed more slowly.

'You noted the registration number?' the Chief Inspector was asking McIver. 'Then get on to Swansea. See what they can tell us.' He turned his attention to us. 'You seem to have been helpful,' he said, as though the fact would be taken down and might be used in evidence against us. 'Perhaps you can help once more. You were wearing full-length waders earlier,' he said to Eric.

'You want me to fetch that rod for you?'

The Detective Chief Inspector looked scandalized. 'That's not how evidence is collected. And one of my men will have to search the bottom to see whether anything else came out of his pockets – or was deliberately dropped to mislead us. Will you lend us those waders?'

'If you think they'd fit any of your men,' Eric said.

The Chief Inspector measured Eric with his eye. 'You have a point.' He turned his glance towards me.

'My chest waders are back at the hotel,' I said. I would have liked to see the lean McIver trying to paddle around in Eric's vast waders. He could easily have fallen into one leg of them and become lost. But in all honesty I had to point out another snag. 'If you want somebody to see the bottom in detail, he'll have to put his face in the water. If you do that in waders, you fill them. So he might just as well start off in swimming trunks – the water's warm enough – or a wetsuit and with a face mask.

'And now, if we can't be of any more use, can we get back to our fishing?'

'No, you can't,' said Fergusson, looking more cheerful. 'My men will have to search the river banks. You've done quite enough tramping around and interfering with evidence.'

26

Eric's placid face showed signs of an approaching storm. 'Now, just a minute,' he said. 'Do you know how much I've paid for this beat?'

'No, I don't,' said the Chief Inspector with relish. I guessed that he was taking his revenge for Eric's remark about the tape recorder. 'Nor do I care very much. However it may look at the moment, there are a dozen possible ways that the man could have arrived here, alive or dead. It's my job to find the truth and prove it. To do that, I have to have exclusive rights,' he smiled grimly, 'fishing rights if you like, to this stretch of the river. And any court in the land will back me up.'

Eric seethed for a moment but none of those present was in any doubt that his argument was already lost. 'How long?' he asked.

'Today and tomorrow should do it. We'll be closing off this road, so don't try to sneak back. And don't leave Granton without clearing it with me.'

'Two days? And who,' Eric demanded bitterly, 'do I see about recovering my wasted money?'

'The police authority might reimburse you if the death turns out to have been accidental, but I wouldn't count on it. Otherwise you could try suing the murderer,' said Detective Chief Inspector Fergusson.

I stepped in quickly before Eric could blow his top. 'Come along,' I said. 'At least you've caught a salmon today, and I'll bet that nobody else can say that. The hotel will be serving afternoon tea soon. That will leave nice time for a bath and a drink before dinner.'

'That part of the programme I could go along with. But,' Eric drew himself up to his full height and glared down at the Chief Inspector, 'if I don't get back on the water by dawn on the day after tomorrow, I'm heading straight for the nearest sheriff.'

A small group was approaching along the river bank, two of them carrying a covered stretcher. 'You do that,' agreed Detective Chief Inspector Fergusson. 'Now go.'

I coaxed the fuming Eric into his vehicle and headed

towards our hotel in Granton on Spey. Eric insisted on calling, without an appointment, to see a local solicitor, who told him to leave the detective chief inspector to get on with it and charged him stiffly for the advice.

It took several drinks, a good dinner and the pleasure of exhibiting his catch around the hotel and receiving the envious congratulations of the anglers in residence before Eric was once again his usual self.

FOUR

In the morning, when Eric's fish had been safely dispatched to Aberdeen for smoking, we bought day tickets for the Association water and spent much of the next day, the Wednesday, fishing close to Granton. Conditions were still unpropitious, the weather bright and breathless and the water low, but Eric was buoyed up by the memory of his triumph. His enthusiasm was brought back to fever pitch by a pull that stripped several yards of line off his reel, but without the fish being firmly hooked.

Back at the hotel, Eric was thoughtful. I had long passed the stage of being fish-hungry. Fresh air, beautiful scenery and the genuine pleasure that I found in the act of casting a line were enough; the thrill of a fish fighting against me and coming at last to hand was a bonus. But to fish all day at great expense for no return was not what Eric had come most of the length of Britain to enjoy.

I left him moodily working his way through the many courses available at dinner while I adjourned to the bar. I was having a quiet pint and a chat about trout tactics with one of the locals when I realized that a figure was standing patiently beside me. It was Constable McIver, looking, in slacks and a sports shirt, almost as schoolboyish as he had when I first knew him. He was carrying a large envelope.

'I'm sorry. I didn't see you, hiding behind my shoulder. You want a word with me?' I asked unnecessarily.

'I was enjoying the respite and learning a lot just from listening to the two of you,' he said. 'But yes. I know you, don't I?' he added to my companion.

'And I know you,' said the other. I gathered that any previous encounters between them had not been social.

Tony McIver was not one to hold a grudge. 'I'll get back to you some time about dapping,' he said.

I made my excuses and we slipped away to a table in a corner of the almost empty lounge. A waiter came and I offered McIver a drink. This was no more than a sociable gesture on my part, but to my surprise he accepted a small dram. Either he considered his shift to be over or else whisky is so much a part of life in the Highlands, and particularly on Speyside where many of the better malts are distilled, that an occasional dram is not counted as drinking.

He laid his envelope carefully aside. 'Mr Fergusson told me to find out whether you and Mr Bell can alibi each other for the whole of Monday and Monday night. Tactfully, he said. The most tactful way I can think of is to ask you straight out.'

That seemed to be a reasonable way of looking at it. 'Monday, yes,' I said. 'Monday night, no. Our rooms are as far apart as I could arrange. Eric is a mighty snorer,' I added quickly before McIver could jump to any more sinister conclusion. 'I don't think we were out of each other's sight for more than a few seconds until about eleven. Then I phoned home as usual and went to bed. Knowing Eric, he was probably in the bar until dawn, swapping drinks with anybody who could keep up with him. Does Fergusson suspect one of us? Or both?'

He produced a small notebook and made a note. 'For the moment,' he said in his careful, Highland diction, 'the Detective Chief Inspector has only your advice plus evidence found by yourselves to suggest that the body was ever moved. Sergeant Lennox supports your view of it. Otherwise, Mr Fergusson might be readier to accept it. Those two have never agreed about anything.'

'So he thinks that one of us went back to the river late, hoping perhaps for a sea-trout or two, and knocked a complete stranger on the head?'

'It is not for me to say what Mr Fergusson is thinking,' McIver said primly, 'but Mr Bell himself pointed out that he had paid a lot of money for the fishing. And there are very few fish about. If he found some unauthorized person landing a fish on his beat, there might well have been a quarrel.'

'There might,' I said. 'But I'm damn sure it didn't happen.'

'I have doubts of it myself,' McIver admitted. 'But my doubts are neither here nor there. By tomorrow, the matter may have resolved itself.' He opened his envelope and withdrew what turned out to be a typed version of the statement that I had made beside the river. 'Would you read this over and, if you agree with it, sign it?'

To be a suspect – albeit in connection with a death which might still be proved an accident – was a new experience for me. I read over my putative statement with care. It was a fair version of most of what I had said. My ums and ers and occasional stutters had been edited out and I was surprised to note how grammatical had been my off-the-cuff ramblings. The document confined itself to my statements of fact and neither my asides to the Detective Chief Inspector nor the occasional inferences that he had managed to drag out of me were recorded. On the whole, I decided, it contained nothing which I might later wish to recant.

I was in the process of initialling each page when Eric appeared, flushed with a surfeit of good food and wine and breathing heavily. 'So here you are!' he said. 'The bar looked empty without you. Good evening, young officer.' He made mysterious hand-signals at the waiter.

McIver seeming stunned by the unconventional greeting, I asked, 'What became of you after I turned in on Monday night?'

Eric's moon-face, usually expressive, remained blank. 'That's none of your damn business,' he said. 'But, if you want to know, I went up not long after you.'

An early night was unusual for Eric but I was not going

to tell that to the police. 'There you are,' I said lightly to McIver. 'Not a trace of an alibi between us.'

The waiter, correctly interpreting Eric's gesticulations, brought three large whiskies. Eric signed the chit. I could see his mind working, beyond the fumes of alcohol. 'They've pinned it down to Monday night, have they?'

McIver hesitated, whether over the drink or the question I was unsure. He compromised by sipping the drink, putting it down on the table as far away as he could reach and saying, 'Monday afternoon or during that night, give or take a wide margin. It is difficult for the pathologist to be sure, the body having been in water for an unknown period and nobody to tell us when he had his last meal.'

Because he had said comparatively little, Eric's statement was a short document and seemed to relate mainly to the finding of the body and the fishing rod. He skimmed through it and signed with a flourish.

McIver got to his feet, leaving the second whisky. 'I'm to tell you that you may resume fishing in the morning,' he said formally. 'So you need not be bothering to take Detective Chief Inspector Fergusson to court,' he added.

'Thank God for small mercies!' Eric said.

Eric, I recalled, had been up and about in good time on the Tuesday morning and in a cheerful mood, which did not suggest a night spent either carousing or down at the river. When McIver was safely out of earshot I said, 'Who or what coaxed you to bed so early on Monday night? Your evening is usually only just beginning to warm up as midnight approaches.' Eric said nothing and glared at me. 'You weren't alone, were you?' I said. More sullen silence. 'I noticed that you were making a play for one of the waitresses,' I said. 'The incompetent one.'

Eric sighed and then shrugged. 'She may get muddled with the vegetables,' he said, 'but she knows her onions.'

My curiosity was piqued, if not my envy. 'You must have hidden charms, to score so quickly.'

'My charms went a lot of the way. Fifty quid went the rest.'

32

It was my turn to sigh. Eric had an alibi. If suspicion remained focused in our direction I would have to bear the brunt of it alone.

The police had released only the news that a body had been found in the Spey, leaving it for the media to assume that the death was a fishing accident. The hotel staff, considering themselves to be far above cheap publicity-seeking, had refused to allow the guests to be pestered by the few reporters who had latched onto the story, but our names had got out and two reporters in succession followed us to the river next day. The second, having got wind of the inquiries the police were making, seemed to have added two and two together and arrived at a hitherto unprecedented total but one which was uncomfortably close to the truth. He was as persistent as a wasp after jam, shadowing us along the bank and shouting questions about the body, its condition, exactly where it had lain and any theories that we might have as to how it got there.

Fishing was impossible in the circumstances. In late morning, we headed for the car with the reporter trotting alongside and still firing questions. We found Constable McIver, now back in uniform, emerging from his panda car.

Eric took the reporter by the arm and walked towards the panda car. When Eric takes somebody by the arm and starts walking, they walk with him. The reporter found himself standing in front of McIver. 'This officer is concerned with the case,' Eric said. 'Ask him your blasted questions. And if you claim to have had an interview from either of us, we'll complain to the Press Council.' He left him there and joined me in the front of his own car where I was opening up the lunch basket.

McIver had his own way of dealing with the Press. 'Show me your driver's licence,' he said, and after noting down the details he looked the reporter in the eye. 'If you are still in sight in one minute's time—'

'You don't want to make an enemy of the Press,' the reporter blustered.

McIver became a different person. 'And you do not want to make an enemy of the police,' he retorted. 'You're local. Try that on and you won't be able to take your car ten yards up the road without collecting a dozen summonses.'

'You said that in front of witnesses. You heard that,' the reporter shouted at us.

Eric cupped his ear. 'What?' he asked.

Tony McIver smiled, but it was not a nice smile. 'Which of us do you think can do the other most damage? In one minute, I shall charge you with loitering, causing an obstruction, interfering with witnesses—'

The list ended at that point. The reporter was on his way.

McIver waited until the reporter's Vauxhall was moving before coming to my window.

'Mr Fergusson says that you may leave Granton whenever you wish,' McIver said. 'Just see that we know where we can get in touch with you.'

'I sense developments,' Eric said with his mouth full. 'Have the dead man's movements been traced?'

McIver glanced around. We were in the middle of empty countryside, the trees a hundred yards away, but there might have been ears beyond the hedge. He climbed into the back of Eric's vehicle and wound up the nearest window, cutting off the breeze which had been cooling my neck. 'You've shown that you know how to avoid talking to the Press,' he said. 'Mr Fergusson might not agree, but I feel that we owe you something. Promise that you won't let on that I told you anything?'

We promised.

'Well, then. The motor-caravan was registered to a man by the name of Hollister with an address in Esher, Surrey. The interior of the caravan was not very informative at first. There was remarkably little personal gear. But there were fingerprints which matched the dead man's, so we

34

persevered. The driver was a cautious man. Under the carpet beneath the driver's seat we found a wallet which contained credit cards and a cheque-book, all in the name of Hollister. One of the counterfoils indicated that a cheque for a three-figure sum was paid to the Seamuir Estate about two months ago. On the phone, after some humming and hawing, the Seamuir Estate confirmed that a man by the name of Hollister had rented their Number Four Beat on the Dee and that the beat had been fished regularly for the past fortnight.'

'Bingo!' Eric said. 'You were right, Wal. The Aberdeenshire Dee it is.'

'That is hardly conclusive,' McIver said sternly. There was a pause while he accepted a sandwich and a spare mug of coffee. 'I have driven over the Lecht and back this very morning with a photograph of the dead man and the Estate Office confirms that this was indeed the man who had been fishing Number Four Beat – but what does that prove? He could have caught his fish on the Dee on Monday and then driven over here, perhaps to keep an appointment with somebody.'

'Somebody who killed him?' Eric suggested.

'Perhaps. Or perhaps not. If we accept that he might have driven over here of his own accord, we have no evidence of foul play. Maybe he fancied casting a fly on the Spey and, seeing a bit of water with nobody there and dusk coming on, decided to chance it. He dropped his knife while tying on the fly which had done well for him on the Dee and then entered the water upstream of the bridge. He fell, hitting his head on a rock, and drifted down with the current to where you found him.'

'And his rod?' Eric said.

'That also drifted down with the current until the butt of it caught up in the weed.'

'I'll go along with that theory if it'll keep you out of our hair,' Eric said, 'but I can't say that I like it.'

'I do not like it very much myself,' McIver said. 'But it is not for me to like or dislike. That is Detective Chief

Inspector Fergusson's business. What I am saying is that there is no hard evidence to the contrary. Tell me why you dislike it.'

'All right,' Eric said. He finished the sandwiches and poured himself the last of the wine while he thought about it. 'He gave himself a long walk from his 'van when he could as easily have tucked it in near here. He wouldn't go fishing with a fish he'd caught earlier in the day weighing down his bag – '

'Unless he wanted to impress a local by pretending to have caught it here,' I pointed out. 'Or even cheat to win a bet. There's a motive for murder, if you like.'

'Just possible,' Eric said, 'but unlikely. You don't cast a line in somebody else's water around here without finding a water bailiff breathing down your neck. And I was the first to take a look at his rod. It hadn't drifted into the weed, it was more as if it had plunged in from above.'

'He could have slipped while wading under the bridge,' I said. 'That could have produced a similar result.'

'Any rocks under the bridge were about three feet below the surface,' said Eric. 'I should know. He couldn't fall through that depth of water with enough force to bash his head in, not unless he came down head first off the parapet of the bridge. And the dent in his skull looked too neat and even to have been made by a rock.'

There was silence in the back. When I looked round, McIver was nodding slowly. 'That is much what the pathologist told DCI Fergusson,' he said. 'And he would have expected to find grit or water impacted into the wound. We have not been able to find a rock to fit the wound or anything like it. The pathologist would not commit himself when somebody suggested a fall against the corner of one of the bridge piers, but there was no sign of blood, skin or hair on any of the corners. It seemed also that the body had lain on its back some time after death, but that could be because it grounded in the shallows before moving on to where you found it.'

'None of that seems conclusive either way,' I said.

'No. There is one more thing. There may be a hundred,' McIver added sadly. 'I'm too low on the ladder to be kept informed. But I hear that the nylon leader had been cut, not broken.

'Ah well, we should know more in the fullness of time. I brought back a sample of Dee water. The pathologist drew off a whole lot of water from the mannie's lungs and we shall have to wait a week at least to see whether the laboratory matches it up with the Dee or the Spey.'

'Or even somewhere quite different,' I suggested.

'Do not say that, even in jest,' said Tony McIver. 'Liaison between different forces can be very difficult at times, so they tell me. Just imagine if it turned out that he was fishing the Dee, died in the Tay and was found in the River Spey. No, it just does not bear thinking about.'

Eric seemed restless. He was disenchanted with fishing, at least on our beat. Apart from dreading the possible mass arrival of the Press, he said, the churning up of the river by searching policemen would have moved any fish that might have been there and with no fish running they were unlikely to have been replaced.

'I'm going back to the hotel,' he said. 'Are you coming?'

'I'd like to give it another hour or two,' I said. 'Are you fit to drive?'

'Of course,' he said. 'I'll come back for you in a couple of hours.'

It was his licence and if he followed his present way of life he was going to lose it anyway, sooner or later. To do him justice, his driving seemed to improve rather than deteriorate after the first glass or two of wine, although the law might not take such an enlightened view of it. I let him go and went back to the river.

By the time Eric returned, I was ready to give up. What little breeze there had been to ruffle the surface had died away and in the barely moving water the almost complete absence of fish was clearly visible. The sun was bright. Salmon, having no eyelids, easily become dazzled and unable or unwilling to see a fly. I had hooked one fish which put up a poor fight and when I brought it close I saw that it had been in the river a long time – a mended kelt, spent and inedible. I detached the hook and wished him luck.

Eric looked more cheerful as he came marching along the bank. He sat down on a tree stump. 'Any luck?' he called.

I waded out of the water, took a seat on a boulder and told him of my lack of progress while I removed my fly, hooked it into my fly-box and wound my line and leader onto the reel.

'Things could be about to look up,' he said. 'You're sure that the Dee would be better?'

'Not a doubt of it. Why?'

'It could hardly be worse. I've been doing some telephoning. The Number One Beat at Strathdee Castle was vacant, thanks to the recession – it's an ill wind and all that. I've booked it for the rest of our fortnight. They tell me that fresh-run fish are being taken above and below.'

Such extravagance was beyond my ken. 'But you've about ten days to go here.'

'And we've already caught the only takeable salmon in the whole damn river. It's only money.'

'Sir, you are speaking of the money I love,' I said. (Eric chuckled.) I had fished the Dee quite often as a guest, usually at the invitation of proprietors hoping for a favourable mention in one of the magazines. 'I think Number One Beat's on the right bank and the trees come down to the river. You'll have to polish up your double Spey casting.'

'You can teach me,' he said hopefully.

'Again? I suppose I can try.' More of the geography was coming back to me. Because rivers form natural boundaries between estates, opposite banks are often in different ownership. 'Strathdee Castle Number One is near Seamuir Four,' I said. 'In fact, I think they overlap.'

'Well, there's a coincidence!' Eric said.

'Coincidence be damned!' I replied. 'You're bursting with curiosity about the late Mr Hollister.'

'Two birds with one stone. It's not every day I find a body. A certain amount of curiosity's understandable. Isn't it?'

'You needn't think I'm going to poke my nose in where the police certainly won't want it while a beat on the Spey and another on the Dee go begging.'

'This beat won't go begging. Young McIver can have the use of it.'

'I doubt if he'll have any leisure until they've closed the file on Mr Hollister.'

'Then McIver can pass it on to one of his relatives and be owed a favour. These Highlanders live by scratching each other's backs.'

I let the slander go by, partly because there was a grain of truth in it. We set off back towards the bridge. My fifteen-foot rod bounced uncomfortably so I stopped to take it down into its three sections. 'Have you given any thought to where we're to stay?' I asked.

'There's a village, Bantullich, with a small hotel.'

'The Seamuir Arms,' I said.

'You know it? I could have saved myself a phone-call. A cousin of Amy's lives somewhere around there so I phoned her. She says that it's all right.' Amy, I knew, was Eric's late wife.

'She was right,' I told him.

'You approve? That's good. I couldn't come driving down here to consult you between calls. I've booked us in from tomorrow. Beatrice – Amy's cousin – says that it's clean and dry and the food's good. Probably what they call "good plain cooking" and supermarket plonk.'

He glanced at me anxiously, but I just said, 'We'll get by.' I can be quite content with good plain cooking and supermarket plonk.

'I suppose so,' Eric said. 'Just as long as it isn't bar snacks by microwave out of freezer. I'll phone and let the police know where we'll be and then we can settle down to enjoying what may be a last evening of the fleshpots.'

We had arrived back at his vehicle. 'You're taking your fleshpot with you,' I said.

Eric heaved himself into the passenger seat. The big vehicle settled several inches under his weight. He patted his stomach comfortably. 'That's true,' he said.

Before driving off I took a last look at the river. Usually the Spey is alive with promise, but for once it was shrunken, lifeless and tainted with tragedy.

FIVE

Granton on Spey may be a handsome old town in lush countryside, astride a first-class salmon river, but for the first time in my life I was happy to leave it behind. Eric was in a similar mood. Squeezed behind the wheel, he had shaken off depression and he even sang tunelessly as he drove.

We left behind the fertile valley of the Spey and climbed towards the heather of the Grampian Mountains. Eric tackled the climbs and swoops of the A939 by Bridge of Brown and Tomintoul and over the Lecht Pass with verve. Some of the gradients were posted one in six, or even one in five.

'Do you think that that motor-caravan could have made it over this road?' he asked, changing into a low gear for a long, steep descent.

'If this chap can,' I said, 'it certainly could.' A Ford Escort trailing a conventional caravan was climbing towards us, puffing steam.

'But can he?' said Eric. The road bent sharply at the bottom of the hill and we looked back. The Escort was still going, climbing into the cloud that draped the mountain tops.

We came down at last into the valley of the Dee, emerged onto the North Deeside Road and turned towards Bantullich. The Dee, when we began to get glimpses of it, seemed to be in a much better state than the Spey, well up and slightly coloured. Coming through the mountains we had left the sunshine behind. The temperature had dropped ten degrees and there was a thin drizzle. Our spirits remained high. The angler is the one sportsman to whom sunshine is a mixed blessing.

An hour and three-quarters on the road from Granton, we pulled up in the yard behind the Seamuir Arms Hotel. The hotel was just as I remembered it, of granite and slate, old but well kept and with the woodwork brightly painted, set back from the village street which paralleled the main road. It was warm with memories of old friends, good fishing and tall stories so that there was a welcoming feel to the place as if I were coming home.

To my surprise Sam Bruce, the landlord, set the seal on my pleasure by greeting me by name – no mean feat after an absence of several years. The bar, he said, was nominally closed during the afternoons but it could be open to residents whenever we were ready.

I can drink beer at any hour. Eric was similar, except that his taste was more catholic and his thirst also extended to wines and spirits. We took our luggage up and unpacked. My room was next to Eric's but the old walls seemed solid enough to exclude the sound of snoring.

A long parcel had awaited me at the hotel. I showered, shaved and changed and then, before we went down again, I had a small presentation to perform. Eric had been a generous host and in addition was paying a stiff fee and I wanted to make up for some of the disappointments. Also, I rather fancied treating myself to a new rod. Keith was not averse to helping himself out of stock and as his partner I felt entitled to do the same. Keith took so little interest in such humdrum tasks as stocktaking that I knew he would never notice, nor be in a position to complain if he did.

When I presented him with the rod that he had coveted, Eric blinked at me. 'How did you manage to get another rod up here?' he asked me.

'When I phoned home last night, I asked Janet to put it on the bus.'

'I didn't know that one could do that. Well, I must say that I'm deeply grateful. Do you want my old rod in return?'

'Keep it,' I said. Frankly, I wouldn't have had it as a gift; and Eric's style of casting tended to be so violent that he would certainly need a spare sooner or later.

We found the bar already open for business. A gloomy-looking man in a thin summer suit was occupying one of the stools and apparently enjoying just the kind of bar snack Eric had foretold, while an untouched drink waited at his elbow.

I asked Sam Bruce, who was behind the bar, for a pint of Special. Eric glanced at his watch before ordering a gin and tonic – a superfluous gesture but one which he always made, although I never detected that it made any difference to his choice of beverage.

Mr Bruce poured our drinks and made a note for the bill. 'Nothing to eat?' he asked.

'We'll wait for dinner,' Eric said. 'We stopped for something at Tomintoul.'

Mr Bruce nodded, indicated the bell and withdrew into the back premises.

The white-painted walls of the bar were hung with sporting trophies. Keith had examined the few guns years before and pronounced them of only minor interest, but Eric seemed fascinated by a collection of ancient fishing rods, some of them so heavy that a strong man must have been exhausted after an hour of casting.

A meticulously hand-drawn and coloured map of the river and its immediate environs hung on the wall beside the outer door and I looked at it to refresh my memory. The map was framed and glazed but it must have been removable from its frame because pencilled information had been added in many hands over the years as to the best salmon lies and the places where notable fish had been hooked.

According to the map, a path began almost opposite the hotel and ran down between a wood and the garden wall of a large house in spreading grounds, to the river, which it crossed by way of a chain bridge. I remembered the house, which was a baronial monstrosity of pink granite, all turrets and crow-steps, and also the bridge, a Victorian suspension affair of iron rods, with pillars on concrete bases and a footpath of timber sleepers. On the far bank, the path became a track which continued through woods and broken farmland towards the South Deeside Road and Strathdee Castle. Our beat, Number One, stretched upstream from the bridge for two long pools, finishing at a sharp bend in the river, and downstream for three pools to where a small burn entered. (In this context, a 'pool' is any stretch of slower water between areas of rapid descent.) I fixed the boundaries in my mind rather than risk being found committing the ultimate sin of fishing in somebody else's water.

The glum-looking stranger had finished his snack. 'You're here for the fishing?' he asked suddenly.

'That's right,' Eric said. 'We've got Strathdee Castle Number One tomorrow and all next week.'

'Then I'm your next-door neighbour. I'm on Number Two Beat, this week and next. Harry Codlington. Call me Harry.'

Eric gave our names and we all shook hands. 'You're here alone?' Eric asked.

Harry nodded sadly. 'For the moment. My pal has a business crisis and had to fly out to the States. He'll be back next week, God and the weather permitting.'

'Is the fishing any good?'

'My beat's not been too bad. I've had four good fish in three days.'

I had turned back to the map. Strathdee Castle Number Two was downstream of our beat, beginning at the mouth of the burn.

'Only three days?' Eric said idly. 'I thought you said you'd been here all week. This is Friday, isn't it? Or have I slipped in an extra day somewhere?'

'Friday it is. But I went over to the Spey on Monday for a casting lesson and to visit some old friends. And I

44

don't count today. Something's been going on here. There were police crawling all over the river banks. They tried to send me away. I told them to go and get stuffed,' Harry added with satisfaction.

'And did they?' Eric asked.

'Not exactly. Not while I was trying to fish. I don't know what they got up to in their own time,' Harry added, without the least trace of a smile. 'But at least they stopped trying to browbeat me. I went on fishing, but between the disturbance and the feeling that I was being watched and eager-beavers asking me if I'd caught anything yet I got pretty fed up, I can tell you.

'It's not the easiest place to cast a line – there are trees overhead or just behind you at most of the best lies, which I suppose is one reason why they're the best lies – and every time I got caught up I could hear some bastard give a quiet cheer. So I packed it in. They tell me they'll be finished by tomorrow. If they aren't, I'll be demanding a refund from the estate.'

'Golly!' Eric said respectfully. 'I wish I'd had your strength of mind. Much the same happened to us on the Spey on Tuesday and Wednesday, but we were soft. I did threaten to take the senior copper to court, but we let them push us off and I never thought of asking for a refund. Are you ready for the other half?'

'My treat,' Harry Codlington said, pressing the bell. He sounded more cheerful now that he had found a fellow sufferer. 'Gin and tonic, was it? And a pint?'

I was still studying the map but Eric accepted on my behalf. On the near side of the river Seamuir Number Four Beat, which had been booked by the now defunct Mr Hollister, ran downstream from the chain bridge. Above the bridge, Number Three Beat began.

'What the hell is going on around here?' Harry demanded of the room. 'Policemen combing river banks and harassing honest fishermen. They wouldn't tell me a thing. Salmon poachers? I hear that your beat was poached a week ago.'

Eric's jaw dropped and his eyebrows went up.

'Poached? The girl in the office never said anything about that.'

'Well, she wouldn't, would she?' Harry said reasonably. 'It isn't the sort of thing they boast about.'

'If it was only netted once, the best lies will have been taken over again by now,' I said.

'He speaks at last!' Codlington said.

Sam Bruce chuckled. 'If you get Mr James onto the subject of fishing, he'll talk all night.'

'That's for sure,' Eric said.

Their comments, of course, left me more tongue-tied than ever.

'I was wondering myself what the fuss was about,' Sam Bruce said from behind the bar. 'It didn't sound like poachers. They showed me a photograph of a man and asked if I'd ever seen him.'

'And had you?' Eric asked him.

'Certainly I had. It was a man who came in here most evenings last week. I never asked his name. Mind you, he was alive then. From the photograph, although they'd tried to pretty him up a bit, I'd say that he'd popped his clogs, but when I asked what was up they told me, more or less, to mind my own business. So I made them pay for their drinks. That was minding my own business, as I pointed out to them, but they weren't amused.'

Eric was too full of inside information to hold on to it any longer. 'His name was Hollister,' he said with a carefully assumed air of omniscience, 'and you'd be right about his clogs. We found his body in the Spey on Tuesday morning. It put us off our fishing, I can tell you, quite apart from there hardly being a fish in the river. I did land one good one,' he added quickly, 'but that seemed to be the only salmon there. That's why we decided to move over to the Dee.'

'What had happened to him?' Harry Codlington asked. He seemed to have been further cheered by the news of another misfortune to somebody else. He was almost smiling.

I shot Eric a warning glance. Despite the interest of the reporters, the press coverage of the death had been minimal. If the police wanted to play it down, it seemed to me that it was not for us to broadcast our inside knowledge.

Eric caught my glance and seemed to interpret it correctly. He choked off what promised to be a lengthy exposition of the subject. 'That's what the police want to know,' he said. 'He could have fallen and hit his head.'

'Or somebody could have dotted him one,' said Sam Bruce. He leaned his elbows on the bar with the ease of comfortable familiarity.

'But why are they searching the river bank here?' Codlington asked.

Eric hesitated. 'Between ourselves, there seems to be a possibility that he died here and was moved,' he said at last.

Silence fell while Harry Codlington and the landlord digested the implications of what Eric had said.

The hour for evening trade was approaching. I saw a pale yellow sports car pass the front windows and heard it draw up in the car-park with a slither on the gravel. Almost immediately, a man in a waiter's grey jacket entered the back bar. He seemed very young but he looked like a rugby-player, self-confident and physically strong. One side of his mouth was badly swollen, which seemed to support my guess. I further guessed that he was a student doing a vacation job.

'I only saw him a few times,' Sam Bruce was saying. 'Alec serves in here during the evenings. He'll remember him. Alec, the gentleman who was fishing Seamuir Number Four – his name was Hollister – turned up dead in the Spey.'

Alec started polishing glasses. 'Is that so?' he said.

'You remember him?'

'I certainly do.' Alec put a glass down carefully on top of his cloth and leaned his elbows on the bar in uncon-

47

scious imitation of Sam Bruce. 'Frankly, if he'd been found in the Dee I could have understood it.'

'What was wrong with him?' Eric asked.

'Nothing, really,' Alec said hastily. He straightened up and resumed his polishing. 'Very quiet man. I thought that he was shy, but there was more to him than that. I gathered that he was staying in a caravan, somewhere across the river. He'd walk over the bridge most evenings, have a single pint while he listened to the general chit-chat without saying more than a word or two, and then he'd say good-night politely and off he'd go again.'

'Then why wouldn't you have been surprised if he'd been found here?' Sam Bruce demanded.

Alec shrugged. 'I don't usually gossip about the customers. You know that, Mr Bruce. But if the mannie's dead ... One evening last week he came in early. The bar was empty – it's like that sometimes in the early evenings before the Aberdeen commuters get home – and he took a little longer than usual and had a couple of nips of whisky. So I chatted to him, drew him out a bit. Well, people come into a pub for human contact and a little conversation as well as the grub and booze, and I look on it as part of the job, if somebody's on his own, to be a pair of ears or whatever else he seems to want.

'He loosened up after a while and chatted away quite pleasantly. Told me that he'd been an overseas branch manager for one of the big banks. Israel, Lebanon, Iran, you name it, he'd been all over. Had several passports, he told me, so that he never needed to let one lot of immigration officials see the stamp of a country they weren't on speaking terms with.

'He retired back to Britain a few years ago, he told me. Apparently, overseas service entitles them to an early pension. He wasn't going to say any more but I went and put my foot in it. Just to break the silence, I asked him whether he was married and what his wife thought of his going off on fishing trips on his own. I think that he nearly broke down at that point but he pulled himself together after no more than a sort of hiccup and told me that he and his wife used to go on fishing trips together but that she'd been knocked down and killed in a London street soon after their retirement.'

I saw Eric's face drop. 'Poor devil!' he said softly. It came to me that he would know better than any of us how Hollister had felt.

'That's what I thought myself,' Alec said. 'I've never known that sort of a loss myself. I hope I never do. I'd have thought that I could imagine what it would be like, but looking at his face . . . no, I couldn't.

'Then on Sunday evening – you know the lull we get between the before-dinner drinkers and the evening boozers on a Sunday?'

'Regular as clockwork,' Sam Bruce confirmed.

'That's when he came in again, bought his pint and went to sit in the corner.

'The only other drinker left in the bar was Imad Vahhaji. He's an Arab, Iranian or some such, who rents a house on the edge of the village. He's over here studying the oil industry and not short of a bob or two by all accounts. His clothes look expensive, and I'd kill to get my hands on that car of his.'

'Nothing wrong with the car you've got,' Sam Bruce said gruffly. 'It's not every student can run a car like that off his grant.'

Alec's eyes narrowed for a moment but he resisted the temptation to point out that he was working to supplement his grant. 'It gets me here and takes me home,' Alec admitted. 'But if Imad offered to make me a present of his car, I wouldn't exactly be insulted. Not by a mile. You don't wash a car like that, you lick it clean.'

'He might even do that. Friendly sort of bloke,' Sam Bruce explained. 'Very anxious for everybody to like him. Always standing his hand.'

'That's the chap,' Alec agreed. 'Usually. He was in his expansive mood that evening. Of course, he'd had a few. Not drunk, just seeing the world through rose-coloured glasses. Amazing how these Arabs take to it as soon as they get away from their strict Moslem backgrounds. He offered the other man a drink but only got a head-shake out of it for his pains. So, when Mr – Hollister, did you say? – went to the Gents, Mr Vahhaji asked me what was up with him. I didn't have any other explanation to offer and I didn't want to leave him thinking that Mr Hollister, who I liked and felt sorry for, was prejudiced against Arabs. So I told Imad about Mr Hollister's wife being dead.

'That seemed to upset Imad. He's one of those skinny Arabs with soft eyes like a spaniel and I'll swear that they were ready to fill with tears. But he was just as interested in Mr Hollister's time in the Middle East and wondered whether he knew his – Imad's – home territory.

'Mr Hollister came back, and on the way by he asked me if there was anywhere he could buy petrol on a Sunday evening. I said that there was only one place between here and Banchory, open twenty-four hours including weekends. Mr Vahhaji said that he'd give him the directions and went over and sat down with him. I didn't even try to hear what was being said for the next few minutes. They seemed to be getting along all right. I don't like friction among the customers. But, next thing I knew, Gulf War Two had broken out. Chairs went flying and, within a couple of seconds, Imad Vahhaji had Mr Hollister by the throat and the two of them were thrashing around on the floor.'

'Aha!' Sam Bruce exclaimed. 'That's what the row was, then. I was out at the back. When I came in, my wife said that there'd been some trouble but you had it under control, so I kept my nose out of it.'

Alec nodded. 'Just as well. The proper drill would have been to stay out of it and call the cops, but they could have done some serious damage to each other by then and anyway they were both well behaved as a general rule, so I got Imad Vahhaji by the scruff of the neck and pulled him off. Then Mr Hollister, who'd completely lost his rag, tried to have a go at Imad while I was holding him, which was a bit over the odds. I fended him off and he took a swipe at me, the innocent bystander— ' Alec touched his swollen mouth '—so I kneed Hollister where it did most good. Imad tried to get in a swift kick or two, so I picked him up by the middle and squeezed the breath out of him. Neither of them seemed to have much appetite for a scrap after that.

'I slung Imad outside and told him not to come back until he'd learned to behave as if he was a gentleman. Then, when he was well clear, I said much the same to Mr Hollister and put him outside and I suppose he went off home to his caravan. I never saw either of them again.'

'Quite right,' Sam Bruce said. 'You did well. That's why I employ you.'

'I've always wondered why,' Alec said. He picked up his cloth and another glass.

'That was Sunday,' Eric said thoughtfully. 'And Hollister was dead about twenty-four hours later. Have you told the police about this? They were making inquiries around the village.'

Alec looked blank. 'I must have been at my digs about ten miles away, studying, while they were doing the rounds here. This is the first I've heard of it. You don't suppose . . . ?'

'You'll have to tell them,' Sam Bruce said.

'I suppose I will.' The young barman was looking unhappy. 'I don't want to. I like old Imad. He may've lost his head once but I can't see him killing anyone. He comes across as having about as much aggression in him as a woolly toy rabbit.'

'You don't know what the provocation was,' Eric said. 'Maybe Hollister refused the head of the family an overdraft while he was managing a branch bank out there. These Arabs remember an insult to the family honour for ever and they count life fairly cheap.'

'You'll have to tell them,' Sam Bruce repeated.

'All right. When I get around to it.'

51

'You just want to give him time to scarper,' said Eric. 'But if you haven't seen him since Sunday he's probably back in the family oasis by now, tucking into the sheeps' eyeballs and bragging about how he smote the infidel. Set 'em up again.'

'Dinner won't be long now,' Mr Bruce said warningly.

'Set 'em up all the same. And let's have a look at the wine list.'

The wine list was short but proved satisfactory.

Other drinkers had begun to trickle into the bar and the subject of mysterious death was allowed to lapse for the moment. We became involved with a trio who had been fishing Seamuir Two all day with only modest success – they had one mediocre fish to show for it plus an unlikely tale about a salmon as big as a submarine which had taken the fly, dragged the struggling angler up the Dee and back again and then broken his tackle just when the battle was almost won.

We were all having a little quiet fun, provoking the loser of the contest into ever wilder exaggerations, when Mrs Bruce made one of her rare appearances from the back premises. 'We're ready to serve dinner now,' she said. 'And is Mr Bell here? There's a lady asking for him.'

Eric was silent. I glanced at him in surprise. He seemed to have shrunk. He recovered his voice with an effort. 'Coming,' he said hoarsely. I would have hung back and let him greet his visitor alone but he grabbed me by the elbow, as he had the unfortunate reporter, and steered me ahead of him into the entrance hall. His grip was firm but I could feel a tremor in his hand. By the time we entered the hall I was expecting almost anyone, a gorgon, a policewoman or a young girl with a very large baby.

But the lady who turned from hanging up a fawn rain-coat in the hallway was none of these. She was plump in the pretty way that some women have, as though the plumpness of near middle age were puppy-fat. Her hair, which was chestnut with a natural wave, was tidy but its forward shape, reminding me of a spaniel's ears, put me in mind of one or two ladies who mistrusted the local hairdresser in Newton Lauder and let it grow until they could visit the city. She was neatly but plainly dressed, and for the country rather than the town, Eric, no doubt, could have explained the difference but I, no expert in women's clothes, could only have said that when Janet dressed that way she was going visiting but not straying far from home, and certainly not to Edinburgh. The plain but polished walking shoes were the only clue I could be sure of. The overall image was ladylike, countrified and somehow just right.

Her eyes passed over me, unseeing, and settled on Eric. She hesitated. Her smile, when it came, was unforced. I felt Eric's hand relax and then let go of my arm.

'It is Eric, isn't it?' she asked. 'I haven't seen you since your wedding.'

Eric took her hand and produced his own flashing smile. 'And you must be Beatrice Kirk. It's rude of me to admit it, but I was stunned by so many names and faces at the wedding that I had no recollection of you at all. I've put on weight since then. That's two black marks.'

Her smile widened. Two such smiles in the confined space were infectious. I found myself joining in.

'And full marks for honesty,' she said. 'You were afraid that I was going to turn out to be a reincarnation of Amy, weren't you? When you came through the door, you looked ready to turn and run. But I do understand.'

'Your voice is so like hers,' Eric said. 'It brought her back. I half expected to see her double standing here.'

'No such luck. Amy was the beauty of the family.'

'I couldn't have born it if you'd had the same looks. They were special to your cousin,' Eric said in a rush. I guessed that he wanted to get the subject out of the way before his voice betrayed him. He remembered my presence. 'This is Wallace James, my companion and mentor.' He let go of her hand at last so that she could shake mine and he went on, 'We were just about to go through for dinner. Would you join us? Or have you eaten?'

She glanced uncertainly at me, wondering whether she

would be intruding. 'Please do,' I said. 'We're beginning to run out of conversation.'

'Then I'd love to. I have a lot of friends around here and we exchange invitations now and again, but I still get very bored with cooking for one.'

We went through into a dining-room which looked out onto a large garden, slightly overgrown and in full flower. The Bruces' daughter, who doubled or trebled as waitress, receptionist and upstairs maid, laid an extra place for Beatrice Kirk. I glanced at the girl and thought that her parents were working her too hard. Eric ordered wine.

To be honest, I was dreading a mealtime conversation devoted to reminiscences of the late Amy Bell, whom I had never met, but that subject was skirted around. Beatrice drew Eric out on the subject of existence as a widower. Eric tried for a light touch, but the lonely aimlessness came over loud and clear. In her turn she told us something of her own life. She had taken an arts degree but had given up a career in teaching to nurse her mother through a long terminal illness. There had been a fiancé somewhere along the way, I gathered, but he had died in an air crash and she had never married. Now alone in the world, she still lived in what had been her parents' retirement home on money that her father had left her.

'You never felt like going back to teaching?' I asked her.

'I've felt like it,' she said. 'But education has moved on and I haven't moved with it. I'm just beyond the age for thinking metric – I was born imperial and I shall be buried in an imperial coffin. I know the wrong languages and I'm past becoming a student all over again. What's worse, I'd be taking a job away from somebody who needs it more than I do. But I can't bear to be altogether idle. I shall just have to make do with charitable works.'

She made the words sound like a joke but I discovered later that, in addition to serving with great energy on the Community Council, she did indeed do a prodigious amount of work for various charities.

Our meal arrived. Eric's fears proved unjustified. The cooking might be plain but it was very good indeed. The Aberdeen Angus steaks were tender and juicy and the vegetables were fresh out of the hotel garden. Beatrice enjoyed the meal but I saw her give Eric a succession of thoughtful looks as he worked his way through an excellent soup, the main course with extra vegetables and two helpings of apple tart with cream, followed by biscuits and three different cheeses.

Bea, as she asked us both to call her, ate more sparingly and she and I were both finished and were toying with the coffee while Eric was still working on his apple tart. The conversation had moved on.

'The Spey wasn't fishing well?' Bea said to me. 'So Eric told me on the phone.'

'Abysmal,' I told her.

'And so you've moved to here. Which beat are you fishing?'

'Strathdee One.'

'That's been doing well this year. Or so I've been told.'

'We heard that it had been poached,' Eric said.

'On Monday night,' Bea confirmed. (Eric caught my eye and waggled his eyebrows. The presence of salmon poachers could shed a new light on Mr Hollister's death.) 'But I believe that they were interrupted before they could get the net out. I heard a van go by and then the uproar and shouting followed only a few minutes later. You'll have to ask the ghillie about it and get him to show you the best lies.'

'I tried to hire him,' Eric said. 'He's tied up with a couple of visiting Americans this week.'

Something wistful in Bea's voice had given me a hint. 'Do you fish?' I asked her.

'When I get the chance. Toby Seamuir sometimes gives me a day when a beat's unlet. I still have my father's rods.' She sighed for the days gone by and then chuckled. 'You'll have to watch out for His Excellency.'

'Who?' Eric and I asked in unison.

'Don't you know about the ambassador?' She named one of the small Arab states which gain an importance quite out of proportion to size or population by being oil rich. 'He rents the big house by the chain bridge and has a lease of Seamuir Number Three for the whole summer.'

Eric had finished choosing his cheeses. He offered the last of the bottle and then emptied it into his own glass. 'They must pay their diplomatic staff well,' he said.

'Probably they do,' said Bea. 'But I believe his family has money and to spare. Selling camels to the oil industry or something. He comes up here some weekends and stays on whenever things have gone quiet in London. In fact, I think he's in residence just now. I heard the helicopter arrive on Monday and I see it's still parked on the lawn. So watch out. His beat overlaps yours, on the opposite bank, but he thinks the whole river belongs to him. He strays over the boundaries when he feels like it, but he hits the roof if anyone encroaches on his water. He has a couple of tough-looking bodyguards who stand around glaring at the dog-walkers and intimidating other anglers into fishing those parts of their beats furthest from his.'

'They won't intimidate me.' Eric frowned at a comparatively inoffensive piece of cheese. 'Do people walk dogs along the river bank?'

'Where else? It's the prettiest walk for miles around, and safer than the road verges.'

Eric looked at me. 'I thought the sound of dogs' footsteps put the fish off. They sound like an otter or something.'

'That's true, if the dog's running loose near the water,' I said. 'But if they hear it come, they hear it go again. I've never found the effect very lasting. You'll have to come and show us the lies,' I told Bea. 'Bring a rod.'

'We're only allowed two rods,' Eric said.

'Why?' I asked.

'It's a two-rod beat. And when the factor asked me I told him there were only two of us.'

'I'll speak to George McPhee, the factor, and see whether he has any objection,' Bea said.

56

'If he does, I won't mind sitting out for a while,' I told her. She patted my hand.

There was a contemplative silence for a few seconds.

'The police have been all over the place today,' Bea said, 'and it wasn't about poaching. There was a rumour about a drowning, but nobody's seen a body being taken away.'

Eric and I exchanged a glance. 'And nobody local has gone missing?' I said. Eric's eyebrows went up again, as well they might, but I felt a reluctance to spread our inside knowledge around for fear either of hampering the police or of dropping Tony McIver into the mire for talking freely to us.

To my surprise, Bea took the question seriously. 'Nobody except one or two oil industry men who get sent offshore sometimes. I don't know much about it – I live across the bridge and the police don't seem to know that I exist – but I'm told that they've been asking about a man who was fishing Seamuir Number Four last week. That's also partly opposite your beat,' she added helpfully.

This was too much for Eric, who had absorbed three gin and tonics and most of a bottle of a respectable wine. 'We can tell you a little more than that,' he said. Three of the other five tables in the small dining-room were occupied by now. He lowered his voice, although the chatter of three shrill women at the corner table would have drowned a pipe band, and embarked on the story of our week. In the telling, he gave me more credit than was due to me for the little help I had given the police.

Bea was a good listener. Most women, and some men I know, would have interrupted the story with questions or exclamations of amazement, but she sat in silence, attentive and still, during the telling and for a minute after Eric had run down. Then she looked around. 'They'll be wanting this table in a minute,' she said. 'There's a quiet coffee room behind the bar. Shall we move in there?'

Miss Bruce arrived to clear the table before we were out of the door.

SIX

Eric paused on the way through the bar. Bea was persuaded to accept a Grand Marnier. I went back to beer. Eric brought the drinks to us in the coffee room, with a large brandy and a cigar for himself. We had the small room to ourselves for the moment. Bea was still thoughtful.

'You seem to be in pensive mood,' I said.

'You've given me a lot to be pensive about,' she said slowly. 'I think I'll have to go and make a statement—'

Somebody knocked on the door. I called, 'Come in,' although it was hardly for us to invite anyone in to one of the hotel's public rooms.

PC Tony McIver, very neat in a grey suit, slipped halfway through the door and nodded to us.

'You heard the man,' Eric said jovially. 'Come and join us. Drink?'

'Well ... '

'Before you decide to be off duty,' I said hastily, 'if you're still concerned with the death of Mr Hollister you'd better identify yourself to Alec the barman. He has something to tell you.'

'Then I shall do that.'

He closed the door behind him. 'It seems,' Eric said to Bea, 'that you'll get your chance to make a statement sooner than you thought. That young man is a police officer, though what he's doing this side of the Lecht I can't imagine.'

'I could make a guess,' I said. 'What are you going to tell him?'

'Let me sit and think it out,' Bea said.

We sat quietly. Eric concentrated on lighting his cigar. When I made a visit to the toilet, Mr Bruce was tending the bar and I could hear voices from the small office behind the reception desk.

Tony McIver rejoined us about twenty minutes later, notebook in hand, bringing a modest half-pint with him and interrupting me in the middle of a fishing reminiscence.

'This is my cousin, Bea Kirk,' Eric said. 'She lives just across the river. We've been telling her all about it and she has some news for you. You're a little off your usual beat, aren't you?'

'More than a little,' said McIver. 'I am by way of being piggy in the middle. I doubt if my superiors would wish me to be chatting so freely – or you either – but the way things are I need somebody to talk with. Here's the way of it. You'll remember that I stuck my neck out and said that the man's death was no ordinary accident. And you, Mr James, said that like as not he'd been on Deeside. And then we found the cheque counterfoil to Seamuir Estate.

'DCI Fergusson is in charge of the case back in Granton but he believes that, if it wasn't indeed an accident after all, the man was killed here and dumped in the Spey. The procurator fiscal, on the other hand, would be quite happy to take it before the sheriff and press for a verdict of accidental death. But Mr Fergusson asked Grampian Police to assist and they put a team to searching the river banks here, without turning up anything of use. They've come to the conclusion that the mannie drove himself over to the Spey and had an accident or was killed over there.'

'With the result that it's fallen through the crack and nobody's doing very much,' Eric said.

McIver nodded. 'Except for me,' he said. 'I'm sent over

here, with the acting rank of detective constable, to liaise with Grampian Police. I'm reporting to a sergeant who is taking his line from his superiors, and he reports to an inspector who doesn't want to know. I think the intention is to keep me busy but out of everybody's hair . . . except that of the long-suffering public.'

'So here you are,' I said, 'a beardless youth in what amounts to sole charge of a one-man murder inquiry.'

McIver scratched his chin, producing a rasping noise. 'Not quite beardless,' he said, 'but nearly so. I have spent half the day inquiring about the salmon poachers. And now we hear about a fight with one of the locals, and an Arab at that.'

'I meant to ask,' Eric said suddenly. 'Any connection between Imad Vahhaji and the gentlemen from the embassy?' he asked Bea.

'Definitely not,' she said. 'Daggers drawn, my dear. Their respective countries aren't on speaking terms, except at the end of a gun.' She turned to Tony McIver. 'What I was going to tell you, or the police in general, was this. Two things. Firstly, I'm told that the dead man's name was Hollister. He was one of those men who move around quietly, speaking when spoken to and never giving a name unless asked, but when I asked him, if we're talking about the same man, he said that it was Robinson. And, secondly, on Monday evening I saw him heading east towards the end of the village where Imad Vahhaji lives.'

'Do you tell me that, now?' McIver said, scribbling busily. 'I shall likely be along to take a formal statement from you another day. For the moment, I think that I should go and visit this Mr Vahhaji.'

'The last house on the left,' Bea said. 'But I don't think you'll find him at home. The "No milk" notice has been hanging on his gate all week. And now, it's time that I was going. Thank you for dinner; you must come and eat with me soon.' She shook hands politely all round and left the room, only to return a few seconds later. 'If you want to ask about the poaching and its effect on your beat, the ghillie and the water bailiff are having a drink together in the bar.'

'Lead on,' said Eric, heaving himself to his feet.

'A moment,' Tony said. We paused. 'I'm supposed to see a . . . ' He produced and riffled through his notebook. ' . . . a Henry Codlington. He is believed to be resident here.'

I could feel Eric's eyes trying to catch mine but I avoided contact. 'If we see him, I'll point him out,' I promised.

Henry Codlington was talking gloomily to Alec the barman at the far end of the bar. The room was filling up and Tony had to push his way through. Friday night is the traditional night for the working man to drink what his wife has allowed him to keep out of his wages or for the office worker to celebrate the end of the working week. There was a rich mixture of accents. Bantullich is at the limit of daily commuting distance from Aberdeen but suits the oil industry workers who fly offshore from Dyce. Most of the English regional accents were represented and several American.

Bea, when she had introduced us to two men who were sitting apart from the crowd, went on her way, murmuring vague promises about seeing us again. The men, at first, eyed us patiently, as if we were necessary interruptions to more important business, but when Eric had called up a large malt whisky apiece they let it be known that our company was now acceptable. Their accents were local.

Bill Gheen, the ghillie employed by Strathdee Castle Estate, was a man of about thirty, round-faced and cheerful-looking despite the remains of what must have been a magnificent specimen of a black eye. He was unknown to me, having taken over the post on the retirement of Archie Struan. As part of the necessary preliminaries, which included polite enquiries as to the season so far, I asked after the old man who had been a friend for many years. He still lived near by and, I was told, had

61

heard of my arrival and expected a visit. The world of salmon fishing is a small one.

The water bailiff, Mr Donaldson – the ghillie addressed him as Ed – was an older man, very lean, with grey hair beginning to thin. He must have been nearing fifty but he looked very fit. The steel in his eye suggested that he would be a hard man in a scrap.

'So you're fishing our Number One Beat from tomorrow's morn,' Gheen said.

'That's right,' Eric said. 'They tell me you're busy with the American visitors, but we'd be grateful if you could spare a few minutes to show us the lies.'

'I will if I can,' he said politely. He leaned this way and that to see whether his clients were in the bar. Apparently they were not. 'Those Americans won't even change a fly for themselves, let alone land a fish. It's nursemaids they need, not a ghillie. I damned near asked one of them if he wanted his nose blown, but he'd likely have taken me up on it. If I can leave them fishing, I'll come and set you right. But Mr James is an old hand here, he'll look after you.'

Eric judged that enough time had been spent on the courtesies. 'Will our beat be fishing all right?' he asked. 'We were told that it had been poached.'

Bill Gheen looked hurt. 'It'll be fine,' he said. 'Not a fish did they get.'

'But if they'd already put Cymag in the water . . . '

The two men smiled tolerantly. Rather than let them think that we were both ignorant I said, 'Cymag only works in small pools, not wide rivers. You'd better tell him about it or he won't sleep tonight.'

Gheen glanced at the water bailiff, who was employed by the river board. Prevention of poaching was his business and he had powers of arrest.

Donaldson glanced from one to the other of us, as if wondering whether information would be put to bad use. We must have satisfied him because he said, 'This is how they work it. A gang is maybe four men. They start downstream. Where there's a wee brig, as here, they'll walk down ilka side; other places, ane or twa men'll wade or swim across, or I've kenned them use a rubber dinghy, taking the end of a stout rope wi' them. The rope's weighted, if that's what's needed to sink it, and it's dragged up the bottom of the river to feel if there's any bad obstructions, or maybe some cleeks.'

'What are cleeks?' Eric asked.

The bailiff sighed. 'I've spent half the day explaining to yon young bobby who sounds as Highland as Rob Roy hissel'. Cleeks are iron bars wi' a hooked or T-shaped top, fixed in the river-bed specially to prevent netting.'

Eric looked worried. 'Don't they ever catch an angler's line?'

'Very rarely,' Gheen said. 'A'most never at this time o'year when you're fishing a floating line. Whiles, a fish'll tak' the line round ane o' them, and then you've got a problem – but that's what us ghillies are for. Onyway, you'll no' be troubled that way in the first pool, because those lads had the cleeks out.'

'If the cleeks are just hammered in,' said Donaldson, 'a strong gang wi' a stout rope can howk them out again.'

'I've told the factor and the laird that, o'er and o'er,' the gillie said disgustedly. 'The only sure way's to set each cleek in a concrete block and tak' a machine down when the water's low to sink them in deep. But the laird'll no' spend the siller unless Seamuir pays half and they've never yet been willing, the both of them, to spend the money at the same time. The matter's been put off and put off.'

'Aye,' said the water bailiff. 'It's a pity, but there it is. Weel now, when they're sure the bottom's free and clear they use the rope to pull the net across and they draw it down the pool and round, sweeping up a'most ilka fish in the pool.'

'It sounds like a lot of hard work in the dark,' Eric said, 'and a high risk of being caught. Is the game really worth the candle? Or are they doing it for the sport of it?'

63

'Wi' salmon the price it is for a pound? And a salmon weighing fifteen or twenty pound or more?'

'But surely they don't get full value for it? They'd be selling it at the back doors of hotels.'

The bailiff grunted. 'Mair often than no', yon fish are at Billingsgate market by the next night. A good evening's work can be worth thousands to them, just thousands,' he said bitterly. 'Compare that wi' the piddling fines the courts impose and the risk of losing a rusty old van and a net you could put in your pouch.' He leaned forward and glared as though Eric and I were to blame for the failings of the sheriff courts. 'The pickings are so good there's a dozen gangs at it. They come from all over, Dumfriesshire even and beyond.' He sounded as though Dumfries was at the far end of the earth.

'What went wrong with their plans on Monday night?' I asked.

Again the considering look. 'I'm no' wanting to say o'er much,' the bailiff said. 'If the gangs kenned a' the ways we have for catching up wi' them, they'd be even wiser than they are and we'd no' stand a chance. They have their sources of information, local men who'll let them ken when the river's full o' fish. Aye, and likely come out wi' them and guide them around the river. Let's just say that we try to have friends around who'll give us a phone if they see movement at night or hear a vehicle go down towards the river at a time when honest folk are in their beds.

'Monday night, I was just thinking of my own bed at the back of eleven when the phone went and a lady was on the line. I'll not tell you who she is, but there's not much excitement in her life so she keeps an eye out for us and maybe she gets a fish or two from the factor now and again in return. She was driving home when she saw the lights of a vehicle turn down the lane, coming towards the river the far side from here.

'I phoned the police, but it would take them long enough to get here and then likely there'd only be two of them at the most. I'm responsible for a good few miles

64

of the river, but it happens I live not far away from Bantullich so I phoned young Bill here and picked him up in my Land-Rover.

'We went in by the same route the poachers had taken. After the first half-mile it's little more than a footpath, but it'll take a Land-Rover. It's the only way a vehicle can get down to the brig. We'd not the least intention of getting into a rammie, just of disabling their vehicle or blocking it in. If I'd a damn bit of sense I'd've stopped short, but you aye think of these things later.

'The track runs downhill a bittie, so I killed my engine and freewheeled maist o' the way. I'd only on my side-lights, so when we came on their van facing us, about a hundred yards back from the brig, I dashed nearly ran intil't.

'We got out of the Land-Rover. I could barely see the van by my parking lights, but enough that I could have stopped them driving it. I aye carry an apple in my pouch' – he patted a bulging pocket of his tweed jacket – 'and if I don't use it I can aye eat it later. Wi' that up his exhaust, he's stuck.

'What I didna' see was that the beggars had left a man on guard. We were just coming to the van when its engine started and it backed awa' towards the brig, going like the clappers of hell and the horn blowing fit to waken the deid. He was a bonny driver, I'll say that for him, backing full dreel on a narrow track in the dark wi' only his reversing lights and his door mirrors to steer by.

'Just seconds later, we heard his doors slam and he was coming back at us. We could've got intil the Land-Rover and locked the doors, but you feel terrible trapped that way. Instead, I locked it up and we went back among the trees.

'That should haud them, we thought, until the police arrived, but no' a bit of it. The van stopped. There was five of them got out and damned if they didn't start to lift the side of the Land-Rover, trying to cowp it intil the ditch.

'Weel, I wasna' for that. It's my ain Land-Rover. What

I should've done was to use my apple, but I was o'er feared for my vehicle to think of it. I rushed out, and Bill wi' me, and we pushed at the other side of the Land-Rover. It was gey awkward, the ditch being in our way, but they couldna' get it o'er. So, next thing, they dropped it and we were in the middle of the very de'il o' a stishie. Ane o' them took a swing at me wi' a priest that'd hae ta'en the heid off me if it'd landed and I'm a' strappit up yet wi' three ribs cracked and Bill got a dunt on the heid that laid him out. Then they turned back to the Land-Rover and cowped it a' together. They must ha'e been strong lads, for it needed echt men to roll it back again.

'They drove past. I just managed to move or they'd ha'e been o'er the top of me, no' that they was caring – I'd recognized some o' them and likely they guessed it. Glasgow way they come from. I don't have their names yet, but I'll catch up wi' them some day and then we'll see who ends up wi' the sair ribs.

'And that's about it a'. It was another three-quarters of an hour afore the police arrived. I'm told that another couple of pools near Drumoak were netted the same nicht, but that's no' on my patch.'

'By the same gang, you think?' I asked.

He shrugged. 'There's no way of telling. They weren't seen. There's plenty o' the beggars. It could've been some o' the others.'

'Was there still a motor-caravan parked not far from the track at that time?'

The two men looked at each other. 'Yon young bobby asked the same thing,' said Bill Gheen. 'We can only tell you what we told him. It could've been there when we arrived, we wouldn't ha'e seen it. By the time the police came, there was no sic thing. There was lights a' o'er the place.'

Eric offered another round, but they refused. They had no more to tell us except for a few tips about the fishing and a few minutes later they left to do a patrol of the more vulnerable stretches of river.

'What do you reckon?' Eric asked me.

'I'm doubtful,' I said. 'The poachers were disturbed, but they managed to get moving in seconds. That doesn't sound as though they had a body to move. And they couldn't have netted two more pools and still had time for a trip to Granton.'

'Drumoak could have been a different gang. Or, dammit, there were five of them. Could three men do the netting?'

'I think so.'

'Well then. Suppose that one man had a car handy.'

'Why would he?'

'I don't know why,' Eric said impatiently. 'Perhaps at least one's a local. Hollister went down to try for sea-trout and met up with the poachers when they'd finished the rope trick but before they started netting. One of them tapped him on the head harder than he meant to. They loaded the body into the van and went back to collect their net and the rope. That's when Donaldson and Gheen turned up. Two of them went over the Lecht to Granton while the others gave themselves a sort of an alibi by poaching two more pools a long way downstream.'

'How did they know that the caravan belonged to Hollister?'

'One of them was local. Or they did a reconnaissance earlier in the week,' Eric said glibly.

I thought it over. 'Fair enough,' I said. 'But why would they move the caravan to the Spey? What good did that do them?'

'How do I know?' he said irritably. 'Maybe they're well known for poaching only on the Dee.'

'And why the Spey? The upper Tay would be on their way home, or some of the lochs.'

'Misdirection,' Eric said.

Fuelled by alcohol and a lack of adequate information we could have kept up the argument until closing time, but we were interrupted by Harry Codlington, who bent down to put his hands on the table. I was about to offer him a drink when I realized that he had adopted his uncomfortable posture in order to glare into our faces.

'Damn you!' Harry said with quiet fury. Even the locals at the next table could hardly have heard a word. 'Damn you both to hell! What business is it of yours if I was in Granton?'

'None at all,' Eric said. 'What the hell are you talking about?'

In his fury, Harry was making the table quiver so that two glasses tinkled together. I moved them apart. 'Don't give me that,' Harry said. 'This afternoon I told you, in the bar here, that I'd been over to Granton on Monday and hardly any time later the police are following me up, wanting to know what I was doing and who I was doing it with and whether anybody can corroborate what I'm telling them.'

'Well, we didn't give you away,' I said. 'Sam Bruce was in the bar, but I can't see that he'd take the trouble either. You only said that you'd gone over to visit friends— '

'And for a casting lesson,' said Eric.

'—and for a casting lesson,' I amended. 'Why would we expect that to give the police palpitations?'

'Then how did they know?' Harry demanded doggedly, still keeping his voice down.

'Probably,' Eric said, 'you parked in the provost's designated parking place and got your number taken. How would we know how they know? And why do you care?'

'Never you mind why I care. I've just told that young bobby and I'll tell you the same, it's nobody's bloody business who my friends are in Granton and I'll thank you to remember that and not to tell tales behind my back.'

He turned and jostled his way through the throng of drinkers, spilling drinks.

'Well, well,' said Eric. 'Well, well, well, well, well!' Which, I thought, summed it up adequately.

SEVEN

Tony McIver did not return that evening. I made my routine phone-call home and took myself off to bed. I woke once to hear footsteps and low voices below my open window, but soon slept again.

While we were browsing through the papers, obligingly if sleepily brought from the village shop by Miss Bruce, over a cooked breakfast served by that same young lady, Tony McIver made his appearance. He took the chair which had been brought to our table for Bea the previous evening and looked pathetic until Miss Bruce brought him toast and coffee.

'Have you been home over the Lecht and back again?' Eric asked him from behind the *Telegraph*.

'No. They found me bed and breakfast in the village here,' McIver said, buttering toast. 'I'm using my own car and nobody wanted to pay my mileage twice a day. B and B worked out cheaper.'

'Was the second B inadequate, then?'

Tony McIver paused with his toast half-way to his mouth. 'It was all right. But it was a long time ago,' he said, with the self-righteous air of one who has been at work early on a Saturday.

There seemed to be no point in opening a conversation with someone whose mouth was now full of toast and marmalade. We went back to our newspapers. Tony ate with dedication. (His boyish appetite brought back the days when I had taught him to fish. I still thought of him as I had then, as Tony, although I hesitated to use his first name aloud. His new status as an officer of the police seemed to transcend the fact that he had once been my pupil.)

Some minutes later we heard him lay down his knife and pour more coffee. 'I've been typing statements and faxing them to my chiefs,' he said, with the same air of virtue.

We laid down our papers again. 'We put in an hour fishing before breakfast,' Eric said haughtily.

This introduced a topic which was obviously important. 'Did you do any good?'

'I had a pull, but he let go before I could hook him,' Eric said. 'There are fish there. It's just a matter of coming to terms with them.'

'That is true?' I said. 'All you have to do is be cleverer than a creature with a brain the size of a pea?'

Eric refused to be drawn. 'What did Imad Vahhaji have to say for himself?'

'Nothing. His house was dark and silent. But there's a Porsche in his garage, I could see it through the window.'

'He's probably been sent offshore,' Eric said.

Tony grunted. 'I've been on the phone to his employers. They haven't seen him since Monday. Probably he has bolted for home. Or maybe not. Are you going back to the river now?'

'That's for sure,' said Eric, folding his paper. 'No salmon makes a fool of me and lives.'

'I can tell you about the poachers.'

'We know about the poachers.'

'Oh. I was wondering,' Tony said, 'whether one of you might not come with me for a few minutes. I phoned the sergeant, but he said to carry on as best I can. He told me that he is going in to Aberdeen for a meeting, but I think that he just wants to start his weekend and not be bothering himself over what he thinks is a red herring. But I want a witness with me, just in case.'

Eric, I could see, was tempted, but the pull of the fish was greater than the attraction of poking his nose into

70

police business. 'I'll come with you,' I said. I looked at Eric. 'You can manage for an hour or two on your own?'

'Of course,' he said, with dignity. 'I hold the stick in my hands and tie one of those hooks with feathers on the end of the string. I'll go and make a start.'

'Don't be an ass,' I said. 'Ready when you are,' I told Tony.

We set off on foot. The day was dry and warm but still clouded, with a light breeze. The morning's mist had lifted.

'I was sent over here to do liaison and collation work,' Tony said as we walked, 'but I seem to be doing every damn job, all at the same time. In between typing statements, I've been on the phone most of the morning. The Met and the local police in Esher were asked for help, and information has been trickling in. It seems that the man really was Hollister, whatever he might have been calling himself. Or, at least, there's a Mr Hollister from Esher seems to have dropped out of sight and he owns the motor-caravan.' Tony slowed almost to a halt and glanced around but the village street was bare of eavesdroppers. 'Somebody else was been making enquiries about him last week. An Arab – from one of the embassies, they thought.'

'Not our local diplomats?'

'They don't know yet. And there's a daughter somewhere. They're trying to find her. She'll have to make an identification.'

'Did his cheque to the estate office have the name of Hollister printed on it?' I asked. 'Or was it on a new account?'

'It had his name on it, but he explained to the estate office. When he arrived the girl asked him, more out of curiosity and to make conversation than for any other reason, how a Mr Robinson had paid for his fishing with somebody else's cheque. He said that the fishing holiday was a present from his brother-in-law, in return for a favour.'

71

'Reasonable,' I said, 'but apparently untrue. So what was Mr Hollister, alias Robinson, up to, apart from fishing?'

'We have not the faintest idea,' said Tony. 'It may be that he has a lady-friend somewhere near by. But Mr Hollister was a widower. He had no need of a false name to protect his own identity.'

'Unless there was an angry husband somewhere who would be on the look-out for the name Hollister,' I suggested. 'Harry Codlington jumped to the conclusion that we told you he'd been in Granton. He seems very touchy on the subject of just what he was doing there on Monday.'

'Then he should be more careful where he parks his car,' Tony said. 'One of the traffic wardens took a note of his number. He was not so badly parked as to be worth a summons, but she noted the number in case he sinned again.'

'We thought that it was something like that.'

'He seemed to feel that I should accept his assurance that he was not there with murderous intent and he took umbrage when I persisted with my questions.' We walked a few yards in silence. 'But,' Tony said, 'there is something I haven't told you which gives cause for worry. The local police say that Hollister had a two-four-three deer rifle registered in his name. There was a half-used box of ammunition for it in his caravan, but no rifle.'

'Probably left over from some previous stalking trip,' I said.

'We hope so. If the daughter doesn't turn up very soon, they're going after a search warrant. If the rifle isn't in his house, it is possible that he may have been killed for it. In which case, who has it now and for what?'

Before I could try to think of an answer to his questions, which were anyway unanswerable, he came to a halt. The scattered houses of the village were giving way to a wood of mixed conifers, beyond which were open fields.

'Last on the left,' Tony said. 'I'm not convinced that he isn't there. It doesn't *feel* empty. I'm going to knock on the front door. Then I'll nip round the back in case he makes a bolt for it. If anyone opens the front door, call me. All right?'

'Almost all almost right,' I said. 'I'm not grabbing a possible murderer. I don't have the authority or the motivation. Or the guts.'

'If he makes a run for it, it will be from the back,' Tony said comfortingly. 'After a couple of minutes, if he's still sitting tight, start hammering on the door.'

The 'last house on the left' had been built later than its old stone and slate neighbours, with a granite front but roughcast sides and a tiled roof that came up almost to a point, so that the chimneys at either end stood alone and phallic instead of growing out of their gables. I thought that it was probably more comfortable to occupy than its neighbours but it looked out of place, like a child among pensioners. The curtains were drawn. A prefabricated garage stood, as though ashamed, to one side in a labour-saving garden which was mostly planted with shrubs and heathers. A neat sign, saying NO MILK, hung on the gate.

A gravel drive led to the front door, but Tony led the way silently across a small lawn. Our footsteps crunched as we crossed the last few yards on gravel.

Without delaying, Tony rang a long peal, rapped with his knuckles and called out, 'It's the police, Mr Vahhaji. Open up, please.' He made a long jump onto the grass and hurried round the corner of the house.

I waited. The house seemed silent but, as Tony had said, it did not feel empty. Perhaps there was warmth or tiny sounds and smells, below the level of conscious perception. The curtains never moved. I was becoming convinced that we were wrong, that Imad Vahhaji was offshore or out of the country, but I followed instructions and hammered loudly on the door. Fists and knuckles produced only a sound muffled by flesh, so I picked up a stone and rapped on the glass panel.

Almost immediately, I heard a voice and footsteps.

The front door was opened by a thin man in his middle thirties with a narrow moustache and curling black hair. In a face that looked no darker than a light tan would have looked on a European, his eyes were large and soft, just as Alec the barman had described them. He was immaculately shaved and even in corduroy trousers, Turkish slippers and a dressing-gown he gave an impression of dapperness. Close behind him Tony McIver seemed to tower, although the difference between them was only a few inches.

In despondent silence, Imad Vahhaji led us into a small sitting-room.

'The time for hiding in the dark is over,' Tony said. He drew back the curtains and daylight swept in. The furnishings were commonplace and had evidently been rented along with the house, but the few personal possessions in the room were obviously of the best. Lights were flickering on a hi-fi set-up that I frankly coveted and the headphones that had been laid on top of it were muttering. Vahhaji's lack of immediate response to our arrival was explained.

We sat down on a small, hard settee finished in moquette. Vahhaji turned off the hi-fi and perched on the edge of a matching armchair.

'You have no difficulty with English?' Tony asked him.

Vahhaji was clearly in a state of apprehension but he managed a small smile. 'I was educated in England,' he said gently.

Tony produced his notebook and opened it on his knee. I noticed that he wrote fluent shorthand.

'You are Imad Vahhaji?'

'I am.'

'I have to ask you some questions about Mr Bernard Hollister. And I must warn you that anything you say will be taken down and may be used in evidence. You understand?'

'I understand.'

'You may have known Mr Hollister as Mr Robinson, but you know who I mean?'

'Yes.'

'You know that he is dead?'

Vahhaji hesitated and then said, 'I had heard so.'

'Last Sunday, the fourteenth, in the evening, you had a fight with him. Tell me about it.'

'It was a fight. We disagreed. If you have heard all about it you will know that no lasting harm was done.'

'But you were the aggressor?'

'Under great provocation!' Vahhaji's fear was transformed to something close to anger. 'I am not a man of violence. I spoke to him in the hotel. I was only trying to be friendly in my clumsy way. The barman had told me something of the tragedy in Mr Robinson's life and I was sad for him. I have known what it is like to lose one who was dear to me. Mr Robinson had seemed a very quiet man, very controlled, but when I spoke with him he heard me out in silence at first, so that I thought that he was listening with understanding. Then he said something so unspeakable, so terrible, so unforgivable that I . . . I lost my head. It was only for a moment and I was ashamed afterwards.' Vahhaji's hands were twisting together and there were real tears in his eyes.

There was a pause while Tony's shorthand caught up.

'You spoke with him again later?' Vahhaji remained silent. 'Come on, now,' Tony said brusquely. 'Mr Hollister was seen walking towards this house late on the following evening.'

'He came to see me.'

'And there was more violence?'

'Certainly not,' Vahhaji said indignantly. 'Write this down, Mr Policeman, it is the truth. He came to me to apologize. He said that he was under great strain and something I had said stung him, as we say, on the raw. But he realized that I had not meant to offend and indeed I was not at fault, and he was sorry for what he had said. And he told me that there was no truth in it, for which I was very much thankful although since then I have wondered whether he was telling the truth or only trying to spare my feelings. It was a most gracious apology, but

75

what he had said was, as I told you, unforgivable, so I said to him that, while I accepted his apology and would not mention the matter to anyone, I would prefer not to speak with him in future. He said that he quite understood and he went away. I never saw him again.'

Tony finished making loops and squiggles. 'What was it that he said to you?'

'I am not saying.'

'It may contain something relevant to my inquiries.'

Vahhaji shook his head violently. 'It does not! It was wholly irrelevant. And, I have already told you, it was beyond repeating.' He paused and lowered his voice, speaking more calmly. 'I have made up my mind that I shall never speak of it again unless I am forced to, and then it would be only in the presence of my solicitor.'

'Who is your solicitor?'

'I shall find one.'

Tony seemed to have run out of questions but it seemed to me, from long experience of cases in which my partner had been involved, that there were one or two loose ends to be tied up. 'You might care to ask him,' I said, 'how and when he heard that Mr Hollister was dead.'

Tony looked the question at Vahhaji.

'Everybody in the village knows it.'

Tony had caught up with me. 'They know it now,' he said. 'But you have been keeping to the house with the curtains drawn, not showing a light or making any noise, for several days.'

Vahhaji drew himself up and tried to thrust out his gentle jaw. 'Arrest me if you will,' he said. 'I am not saying any more. I have told you the truth. He spoke the words which began the trouble but mine was the first physical violence. I accept that. But nobody was hurt.'

'Alec, the barman, seems to have taken a punch in the face,' I remarked. 'Was that from you or from Mr Hollister?'

Vahhaji shook his head so violently that I thought he would do himself an injury. 'Why would either of us hit the barman? He was unmarked.'

'It shouldn't be difficult to find out when Alec first showed signs of bruising,' I pointed out to Tony.

'He did not receive any bruises at my hands. Nor at those of Mr Hollister. Unless . . . '

'Unless what?' Tony demanded.

'Unless there was more trouble when he went back . . . '

'He went back? To the inn?'

'I am assuming so. After we had spoken, it was time for the hotel to close. He looked at his watch and said as much. He said that he would have to hurry if he was to catch the barman. I assumed – I still assume – that he intended to offer the man just such a gracious apology as he had made to me. That is all I know.' And no further questions could extract any answer from him other than a shake of the head.

'I don't want to have to take you into custody,' Tony said at last. (My guess was that he was uncertain of his powers.) 'Not unless you force me to. I suggest that, for the moment, you voluntarily surrender your passport to me.'

Vahhaji willingly produced his passport from a crocodile-skin briefcase and handed it over. He came with us to the door. 'I may go to my work on Monday?' he asked.

'Yes. But don't go offshore without speaking to me first.'

'I never go offshore. I have not yet passed the course.' Vahhaji peered cautiously through the door. The road seemed deserted. 'And, please, I do not wish the local people to know that I am here.'

'Why not?' Tony asked quickly.

But the door was shut firmly behind us and a few seconds later the curtains were closed again. Tony hesitated, on the point of going back and demanding an explanation, but he shrugged and came away.

We walked back along the nearly empty street. A van went by and up ahead two women were pushing prams, but otherwise we had the place to ourselves.

77

'Now they will just have to put some men back on the job,' Tony said. 'It was all very well, leaving me to waste my time here alone. But now . . . It has the makings of a strong case.'

'Against Vahhaji? If poachers were duffing up the ghillie and the bailiff and if Hollister's rifle was stolen and if the barman who had already had a dust-up with Hollister collected a battered face, all in the same area and on the same night, the defence could present several good red herrings.'

'If we don't find more evidence,' Tony agreed. 'We don't know yet that the rifle is missing nor, if it is, where it was stolen. But the point is that there was a fight just before the man died. House-to-house inquiries will have to begin again. Somebody must know whether Mr Hollister left Vahhaji's house alive and whether he went back to the hotel and whether Vahhaji went out again that night.'

'Do you really see the Arab as a murderer?' I asked.

'That is neither here nor there. On the basis of five minutes' acquaintance, I can imagine him finding a polite excuse to avoid a fight, or just plain running. Frankly, I am surprised that Hollister managed to lay hands on him at all. But the mildest of men can become tigers when given enough provocation. Only the evidence counts. There was a fight. They met again. One of them has died.' Tony was silent for a few yards. 'I wonder what it was that Hollister said.'

I was wondering the same thing. If there were magic words to reduce an opponent to a state of gibbering fury in a matter of seconds I would have liked to know them, if only so that I could say them to Keith when he was at his most irritating.

We stopped our discussion as we passed a group of ladies chatting at the door of the village shop, a converted cottage which looked as though it could do no more than satisfy the villagers' most humdrum daily needs but which in fact carried a remarkable range of hardware, clothing and . . .

'Food,' I said suddenly as we drew clear.

'You surely can't be hungry again already.'

I ignored the irrelevancy. 'You entered through the back door of Vahhaji's house. Did you see a freezer?'

'No. There was a fridge. They usually have a freezer compartment. Why?'

'Vahhaji wasn't expecting a quarrel,' I said. 'Nor a second encounter. He knew that Hollister was dead, either because he had killed him or because somebody told him. He – Vahhaji – decided to stay indoors and keep his head down until he heard that it was safe to emerge. But heard from whom?'

'I think that I see what you mean,' Tony said doubtfully.

'What I mean is this. Vahhaji wouldn't have been expecting to be housebound for most of a week. And it doesn't look as though he's been out and about during the hours that the village shop has been open.'

'He's thin. He could have been getting by if he had a loaf and a few tins in the house,' Tony said.

'Perhaps. But I think that somebody has been feeding him. I heard noises in the night around the hotel. So I'm wondering if the same person hasn't been feeding him information as well as good plain cooking.'

'If he was the killer, he wouldn't need information,' Tony said doubtfully. We walked a few more paces in silence. 'Who could it be?'

.'That's for you to find out. But,' I said, 'you might start with the daughter of the house.'

'Which house?'

'The public house. I thought that she was looking nervous, but I hadn't set eyes on her since she was a teenager and maybe she always looks like that. Then at breakfast this morning she looked at though she had been short of sleep; and she has just the plump, blonde prettiness that sends them mad in the Middle East.'

'Oho!' Tony said. He looked round at me sharply and walked into a forsythia which overhung a garden wall. 'Dash it,' he said mildly. 'I must see the young lady and then use the telephone, in the hope that any one of my myriad of superiors is working today.'

'You have your kind of fishing,' I said, 'and I have mine.'

'I would happily exchange with you,' Tony said gloomily as we entered the hotel.

We parted in the hall. I collected my new rod and other gear. Waders are easier to wear than to carry, so I donned my chest waders and waddled off towards the Dee.

The path to the river began as a narrow slot between two houses and then opened up into a broad track sloping down between a wood of mature conifers and a granite garden wall. The height of the wall cut off the view of anything but the highest treetops in the spacious grounds, but when I reached the chain bridge I glanced back. The ambassador's house – which had once been occupied, I remembered, by a charming old lady who loved to enter-tain visiting fishermen to drinks and snacks on the lawn – was a large and rather rambling dwelling set in several acres of walled garden. It was just as I remembered it except that the old lady would never have tolerated a small helicopter on the lawn.

Further down the pool that began at the bridge, two figures were standing close together in the water near the south bank. The one which towered above the other was easily recognized as Eric but it took me a few seconds to realize that the other was Bea, looking very masculine in chest waders, a plaid shirt and an old fishing hat. Their hands were locked together on his salmon rod and she seemed to be instructing him in a tidy switch cast.

Making way for a woman with two German Shepherds on leads, I completed my crossing of the bridge, descended to the river bank and followed a path made by a thousand fishermen and dog-walkers beneath the overhanging trees until I came abreast of the two anglers, where an old but well-varnished split cane rod was safely propped against a tree. I sat down on a root with my back to a sturdy trunk and prepared to comment favourably or otherwise on the lesson. A warm breeze was tracing patterns on the surface of the water and keeping the midges at bay, but whenever the breeze dropped the midges swarmed to the attack. I dug in my fishing bag for the Jungle Formula.

The murmur of a river, with quiet voices and the occasional swish of a cast, is as soporific to me as the sound of a distant cricket match. And I had been up early. I was on the point of dozing off before the pair in the water realized that I was there.

Bea waded ashore. 'You don't have to let me spoil your fun,' she said earnestly. 'We're only using one rod and, anyway, Johnny said that three rods would be all right as long as I was one of them and nobody on the other bank objected.'

The late Mr Hollister, alias Robinson, had been fishing the opposite bank. 'As long as at least one of us stays below the bridge,' I said, 'there's nobody in a position to object. I'll go and try a cast or two further upstream.'

Eric was still thigh-deep in the river but he was listening. 'Fair enough,' he said. 'Did you find Imad Vahhaji at home?'

'He was at home all right,' I said. 'Don't let Tony McIver know that I've talked out of school, but Vahhaji says that Mr Hollister only came along to apologize.'

'I could believe that,' said Bea. 'From the little I'd seen of him, he seemed to be that sort of man. Friendly but apologetic with it, like a spaniel that's unsure of its welcome.'

'Vahhaji refused point-blank to say what the row was about. He also said that he'd prefer that nobody around here knew that he was at home.'

'I wonder why,' Bea said, frowning.

'He wouldn't say,' I told her. 'Offhand, I could only make a wild guess.'

'You tell me your wildest guess,' Eric said, 'and I'll tell you mine.'

'No deal,' I told him. 'I came for the fishing, not for fruitless guesswork.'

Irritated, he mistimed his cast and wound the line round his rod. I picked up my bag and the new rod and walked back to the bridge. To avoid the winter spates, the bridge was set high above the water. Rather than climb the steep slope up to the main footpath and down again, I pushed through the weeds that grew on the bank between the water's edge and the concrete base below the pillars.

Half-way up the next pool, several rocks showed above the water and swirls on the surface showed the position of others. These would provide perfect small areas of slack water where a travelling salmon might rest and indeed the map had shown favourite lies in the vicinity. I tied on a Waddington, waded in further up and began to cast across and downstream.

Because of the slope of the ground opposite, my new position gave me a good view of the wide granite house and its spreading garden. Movement caught my eye. Two men came out of the french windows and walked down the garden past the resting helicopter.

At my second cast, a fish took hold and drew out a yard of line. I waited for it to turn before striking, but the line went slack. I made a note of the place to try again later, moved a yard downstream and cast again.

Casting downstream to one's right can pose a problem for right-handers but the lack of three fingers from my right hand has forced me to be largely ambidextrous. As a result, I can change hands and cast off either shoulder without difficulty. But the woman with the dogs was on her way back and had lingered while one of them anointed a corner of the garden wall. Harry Codlington, in waders and carrying his fishing gear, had paused on the bridge to glare at me. I could see Bea and Eric through the bridge and I thought that they were watching me. The two men had come out of a gate in the wall onto the opposite bank and another had emerged from the french windows. The place was becoming as crowded as a shopping centre in the week before Christmas.

With so many eyes on me, I was tempted into using the double Spey cast, a showy cast which looks both elegant and skilful when performed properly. The perfect figure of eight drew itself in the air, the fly brushed the water, but just when the line should have rolled out across the river the hooks caught the one twig that reached far enough over the water.

The woman walked on. Harry sent a sneer in my direction before following. Eric and Bea turned away, no doubt laughing. Feeling the complete idiot, I set about recovering my line.

Controlling a fifteen-foot rod while trying to pull down a springy branch and then get hold of it to detach a barbed hook which has whipped several times around it and taken a good grip on a twig calls for more fingers than I possess. Indeed, a third hand would have been useful and a fourth would not have come amiss. It was several minutes before I had the line clear and was able to reel in.

After so much disturbance, any fish remaining nearby would have been put off taking for some time. Deciding to move to the next pool upstream and work my way down again, I waded out.

The two men from the big house had crossed the bridge and were waiting for me. They were dressed in neat suits with white shirts and their ties were suggestive of the better sort of club, but there was no mistaking what they were. Their skins were dusky and their noses were proudly hooked. They were Arabs, but of Bedouin origin, North African rather than Middle Eastern. They would have looked more at home with a camel, a burnous and a snaphaunce jezail apiece.

But their English was good. The taller of the two spoke first. 'What are you doing here?'

Usually, I take people as they come, be they black, white or purple. If he had spoken to me with even moderate courtesy I would have responded in kind and have forgotten almost immediately any racial difference between us. Conversely, any equally arrogant but stupid question would have put my hackles up coming from an English duke, and had done so in the past.

'I am knitting a hang-glider out of barbed wire,' I said slowly and distinctly. 'What are you?'

They were both large men. The less tall, but distinctly broader, companion of the first speaker pushed forward. His suit, I noticed, had come off the peg and it only fitted where it touched. 'You are trying to be funny?' he demanded.

'Yes,' I said. 'Are you trying to be clever?' I also invited them to go away. There are ways and ways of telling somebody to go away, and I chose the rudest that I could call to mind in the heat of the moment. I do not take kindly to being pushed around.

The expression that I had used, which might well have been incomprehensible to a delicately reared Briton, seemed to be within his comprehension of the English language. I thought that he was going to hit me and I prepared to toss my rod out of harm's way and reverse into the river, pulling him in with me. Nothing takes the fight out of a man like finding himself fully dressed in cold water. They were beginning to crowd me but the taller man put his hand out to restrain his companion and said something soothing in Arabic.

'Who are you?' he asked me.

'None of your damned business,' I said. 'Who are you?' Even as I spoke I thought that it was a question almost as stupid as their opening gambit. I could guess perfectly well who they were.

Somebody disagreed. 'Good question,' said another voice. We all looked round. Tony McIver was approaching from the direction of the bridge. Despite his youth he managed to exude an air of calm authority. They stepped back and we waited in silence until Tony reached us.

'I am a police officer,' he said, rather grandly. He waved an identity card but I noticed that his fingertip concealed any mention of his lowly rank. 'I know Mr Wallace James and I know that he has a permit to fish this beat. Now

84

let's get back to his question. Your names?'

The taller man, as well as being much the better dressed, seemed to be the senior and the more diplomatic. 'I am Ibrahim Imberesh,' he said, producing a smile which struck me as seeming spontaneous by dint of a great inner effort, like the practised smile of a dancer in mid-lift. 'This is Ali Bashari. We are responsible for the security of His Excellency Abdolhossein Mohammed Flimah.'

'The ambassador?'

'Exactly so. It is our duty to know who is going about within gunshot of His Excellency. Truly, officer, there was no call for unpleasantness. Mr Wallace James need only have explained what he was doing here, on His Excellency's beat.'

'His Excellency's beat is on the other bank,' I pointed out.

'But you were fishing much of the way across the river,' Imberesh said.

'That is quite usual,' I said patiently, 'especially when the other bank is unoccupied. When His Excellency fishes from his bank, he's welcome to cast his fly across here.'

'You are very kind,' said yet another voice. The third figure had emerged from the gate onto the further bank and his voice came clearly across the water. The two bodyguards stiffened and bowed their heads in what was almost a salaam.

His Excellency was shorter than his employees and much more rotund but he had the same dusky skin, proud nose and dark, hooded eyes. He was dressed and equipped for fishing and even from a distance I could see that his gear was expensive and nearly new. He fired off a burst of Arabic which caused his henchmen to flinch.

'Please ask your men to open their jackets,' Tony said. 'I wish to be sure that they are not armed.'

'Let it be so,' said His Excellency, and it was so. 'I shall go up and start from the head of my beat,' he continued smoothly. 'You may fish your own beat here in peace, Mr Wallace James. I had word that you were here. I have read your words of wisdom with great pleasure. I enjoyed your article on early season nymphing in the current issue of *Salmon, Trout and Sea-trout* very much. In fact, you may fish from this bank if you wish. You may manage better. There are fewer trees to interfere with your cast.' And he set off upstream, probably chuckling to himself, leaving me ready to grind my teeth. A diplomat, I supposed, becomes adept at choosing the most effectively barbed insult and slipping it into the conversation as if by accident.

'We shall be watching you,' Imberesh said. The look he gave me suggested that, whether or not his master had offered me the hospitality of the other bank, I would be very rash to accept it.

Refastening their jackets, the two bodyguards faded into the trees, keeping pace with their master on the other bank.

EIGHT

I relieved my feelings by wading into the water and repeating the double Spey cast. This time it worked to perfection and I felt better, although my audience seemed to have melted away. Tony was looking gloomily after the retreating backs. 'I would have liked the chance to ask a few questions,' he said. 'That house has a grandstand seat overlooking the bridge and an oblique view of most of the beat the late Mr Hollister was fishing.'

'Not a good time,' I said, wading out again.

'No. Confidential investigations are not conducted by shouting across a river. Unfortunately, the inspector already made a clumsy approach to them and they retreated behind their diplomatic immunity. I shall have to ask that somebody more senior makes a formal request for an interview. Foreign diplomats have to be handled with care.'

'Not by me.'

'So I noticed. I never realized that you had such a short fuse.'

'It's a long fuse,' I told him. 'Very long. But there's more than a little explosive on the end of it. I was about to move anyway,' I added as I finished reeling in. 'The splashing and arguments will certainly have put the fish down for the moment. His Excellency's gone upstream so I think I'll try further down.'

We trod the narrow path in single file and passed under the bridge. Eric was fishing near the tail of the pool under the eye of Bea, who had taken a seat on the bank.

87

We joined her. Bea and I, being in waders, could sit comfortably on the bank with our feet in the water but Tony had to perch uncomfortably on an uneven rock.

'Eric's casting better,' I said. 'Apparently he listens to you.'

'He pays attention to my voice,' she said seriously, 'because it resembles Amy's. How are you getting on?' she asked Tony. She treated me to a wink from the eye that he couldn't see. 'Or shouldn't I ask?'

'Ask away. I seem to have few if any secrets from your companions and you've already been of more help than most of my colleagues. It was you who told me about Mr Hollister visiting Vahhaji. Also, you may be able to help some more. You know the area and the people.'

Bea waited for him to go on, but evidently Tony was expecting more specific questions. 'Did you find Imad Vahhaji?' she asked.

'You haven't heard?' Tony gave me an approving but undeserved glance and went on to explain briefly what had happened at Vahhaji's house. 'Mr James suggested that the girl at the hotel, Jean Bruce, the landlord's daughter, might have been feeding him and keeping him informed. I have just seen her. She was getting upset until her father stormed in and told her not to answer any more questions, which was quite unnecessary because up to that point, apart from denying that she had ever even met Vahhaji, she had not answered any.'

'Well that, at least, is nonsense,' Bea said. 'I've seen them together, walking by the river hand in hand. Not very often, because their leisure hours tend not to coincide, hotel work being what it is, but I've seen him in the hotel mooning over her. Mooning in the British sense, not the American,' Bea added hastily, in case we should suspect Mr Vahhaji, in addition to murder, of baring his behind at the girl. Bea looked at her watch. 'I'll have to go soon. Can I leave my trappings with you and come back later?' she asked me.

'Yes, of course,' I said.

She got to her feet and began to work out of her waders, revealing a pair of trousers which, to my surprise, were not as unflattering as trousers usually are on the fuller female figure. Although she was plump, her plumpness was evenly distributed and she had not run to hips and thighs. Eric was visibly impressed.

'You leave Jean Bruce to me,' she told Tony. 'I was her teacher when she was in Primary and she still treats me as though I'm going to give her lines for inattention. I'll get the truth out of her. And I can deal with Sam Bruce any day of the week.'

In the face of such confidence, Tony McIver could not protest. 'I just hope that you can,' he said. 'I have been on to Aberdeen. The day being Saturday, the officers on duty were not the ones I should have been speaking to and I found myself connected to a very senior officer, a detective chief superintendent, no less,' Tony said respectfully. 'He had me tell him the whole story. He agrees that I have something. Not enough to bring a whole lot of men back on weekend duty, but he promises some officers for house-to-house inquiries on Monday and in the meantime if he can clear his desk he will come through here – not, I think, to look into the case but to see for himself what the middle ranks have and have not been doing. Well, I for one do not intend to cover up for them. I think that Traffic Division may be due for a sudden influx.'

'I should think so too,' Bea said severely. She arranged her rod and waders in a neat group.

'So,' Tony said, 'I would like fine to have made some progress before he comes.'

'Yes, I can see that that would be a feather in your cap. I'll have a word with the girl and point out that she's doing her boyfriend no good and probably a lot of harm by being evasive. She'll believe it from me even if she might not from you. What else do you want me to tell you?'

'I want to know who I should speak to. This area, around the bridge, is constantly trodden by dog-walkers.

To save me from having to stand here all day accosting them, tell me who they are.'

'I can give you a few names,' Bea said, 'but why not start with me? I live this side of the bridge but all my friends are in the village, I shop there and I sometimes have a snack at the hotel to save cooking for one. I suppose I walk over the bridge as often as anybody.'

'You used to see Mr Hollister fishing?'

'Often. He could cast a beautiful line. And when I met him walking between his caravan and here we usually stopped for a few words about the weather or the fishing. His path from where he kept his caravan joined my path from the house. He seemed very agreeable,' Bea added. 'Not at all the sort of man to get into a fight in a pub. But I thought he was nervous, although I couldn't tell you why I thought so.'

Tony hesitated but moved on. 'Was he ever carrying anything?'

'Just his rod and fishing bag, and occasionally some shopping.'

'When did you last see him?'

The breeze had fallen away for the moment. While she considered her reply, Bea flapped ineffectually at the midges. 'He was fishing for most of Monday. I crossed the bridge half a dozen times and he was always in view. He seemed to have taken a fancy to this pool. Once, he had a good fish on the bank. He held it up for me to see and I gave him a little round of applause. I'm sure that it was Monday, because I was invited for after-dinner drinks with friends in the village and on my way home, around nine, he was still there.'

Tony McIver was nodding. 'So he was there until nine at least.'

'He'd left the river by ten,' Bea said, 'although I'd seen him fishing very late on other days, probably hoping for a sea-trout. I'll tell you how I know. I got home, washed up the dinner dishes which I'd left soaking in the sink and when I went to put my things away I realized that

I'd dropped one glove. I don't so much mind losing a pair if they're not too expensive, but when you lose one glove the other always looks so forlorn and reproachful that I never have the heart to throw it away.'

'And if you do, the first one turns up again,' I said.

'Exactly. I have a whole drawer full of single gloves, if you know any one-handed ladies.

'So I went back to look for it. He must have gone back to his caravan in the meantime because that's when I saw him walking ahead of me towards Imad Vahhaji's house. That was about ten o'clock. I found my glove almost on my friends' doorstep and they came back from walking the dog and dragged me inside for another cup of coffee. I couldn't see anyone fishing on my way back, and you can see quite a long way down the river from the bridge, even in the dusk. If he wasn't fishing the furthest pool on his beat, he must have still been in the village.'

'Or gone back to his caravan,' Tony said.

'But he hadn't.'

'He needn't have met you on the path. He could have walked home while you were having your last coffee.'

'The daylight was going,' Bea said. 'The caravan or its lights were in full view from the path. If he was there, he was sitting in the dark.'

Tony whipped out his notebook and began to jot in his shorthand. 'The caravan was still there?' he said. 'Between nine and ten on Monday?'

'Definitely.'

'Have you any idea at what time it left?'

'I . . . I don't think so,' Bea said thoughtfully. 'I heard vehicles later, around midnight, but I think that was the poaching incident.'

I lost track of whatever else they said. In moving water, each submerged rock makes a break in the pattern on the surface. When any such break is on the move, there is a salmon below it. Over the years I had got into the habit of watching the surface of a river, and there was a fish coming up towards Eric now, I was sure of it.

'Eric,' I called softly, 'cast straight downstream.'

His cast was slightly mistimed so that his line had a definite snake in it, but that was all to the good. As the line straightened, it would be allowing the fly to drift naturally.

The line straightened with a jerk as the fish took the fly and turned away. Eric pulled – too soon, I thought, but the fish was well hooked. By the time he had brought a fifteen-pound salmon over the net, the best fish of his life so far, Bea had gone on her way. But Tony McIver waited raptly to see the fish brought to the bank and was nearly persuaded to try a few casts on his own account before remembering his duty and dragging himself away.

Bea rejoined us later, looking thoughtful and saying very little. She would, if pressed, have told us the outcome of her talk with Jean Bruce, but if she was reserving it for Tony's ears that suited me well enough. As I had told Eric, I had come to fish, not to take a ghoulish interest in a probable accident, possible murder and just conceivable suicide. Chat and fly-fishing do not mix well. Eric, who had again hooked but this time had lost a good salmon, fished grimly on, refusing even to stop for lunch.

By early evening, when the clouds had cleared at last and the sunshine was painting the countryside in its true colours, Eric had another and smaller salmon, I had four and Bea two, all fresh run with the sea-lice still on them. It was not a big bag by some standards but it had been a bonanza day the way the Scottish rivers had been fishing that year. I gave my catch to Bea. She had few enough chances to put salmon in the freezer while we still had a week to fish. (I had a suspicion that the weather was changing and that during the next week any salmon caught would be hard earned, but I held my peace.) Eric clung to his trophies and his dreams.

Bea set off for home. We dawdled across the bridge, enjoying the sunshine. Even after the sun came out, we had spent much of the day in the shadow of the trees.

'Weren't you curious about Jean Bruce's story?' I asked.

'I was a damned sight more curious as to where my big fish had got to,' Eric said. 'My hour for nosiness is only now approaching. With a little sherry and a lot of coaxing, Bea will spill the beans. I've asked her to join us for dinner.'

'Again?'

'She wanted to invite us to have dinner at her house.'

'Well then – '

'She was telling me that I should lose weight,' Eric said peevishly. 'She's probably into the new cuisine.'

'She doesn't look as though she goes in for the new cuisine,' I said.

'Perhaps she has a weight problem. Glands or something. I missed my lunch. At the hotel, I can eat what I like.'

'She could be right,' I suggested, with all the carelessness of the naturally slimline. 'Maybe you should lose some weight.'

'What for?'

'To live longer.'

'The last thing I want is an interminable old age,' he said gloomily. 'When the quality-of-life curve and the aches-and-pains curve begin to converge, it's time to go.'

'For your sex-life, then. It isn't every woman that wants twenty-odd stone of flab bouncing on her.'

'That's true. I don't know how you do it,' he added, more gloomily than ever.

I thought that he was still on the same subject. 'Do what?' I said.

'Catch all those fish. You didn't seem to spend more than an hour or so fishing. I swear I do everything exactly as you told me, but the beggars avoid me like the plague.'

'Perhaps it's the size of your shadow,' I said lightly. But then I relented. We had come fishing to take his mind away from his loss and loneliness and it was one of those

beautiful evenings that turn the mind towards thoughts of kindly deeds and words. 'Partly, it's knack,' I said. 'But part of your problem is that you don't use your eyes. And you never use the Polaroid glasses I sold you.'

'I never get to use half the stuff you've sold me,' he said, still dispirited. 'Like the net and the priest and the disgorger.'

'And why do you suppose that is?'

He thought about it. 'Because I never catch anything except when you're with me.'

'And that's because I have to tell you where the fish are. Put on those Polaroids.'

We had drifted to a halt near the village end of the bridge. We put down our burdens and he dug his glasses, slightly bent, out of the bottom of his bag. Out of long habit, I was wearing mine.

'Now look into the river,' I said, pointing downstream. 'Never bother to cast to a fish you can see, except upstream – if you can see it, it can see you. But it's a great help to know where they are. Now, what do you see?'

'Damn-all,' he said, but he was beginning to sound interested.

'All right, they're well camouflaged. Sometimes, the first thing you see is a sliver of the pale underside. Or the shadow. But a fish is a different shape from the rocks on the bottom. Watch for that difference, especially a long shape that's aligned with the current at that particular spot. Look in the places you'd choose to rest if you were a fish, wherever the current slackens. And be alert for any slight movement. Rocks don't move. Next time you fish, cast to those places.'

He stared into the water, which was clearing as the level fell. The breeze, which had ruffled the surface and hidden our threatening shapes from the fish, had fallen away. From our high viewpoint and with the reflections removed from the surface by the polarized glasses, every stone on the bottom was outlined in its own shadow. I could see three salmon.

'The flat rock that just shows above the surface,' Eric said at last. 'Is that a fish, just this side of it?'

'He's found a comfortable bit of slack water, where the current divides. Now see if you can spot another one.'

This time the silence only lasted for a few seconds. 'I think I'm getting the hang of it,' Eric said. 'Near the left bank there's a patch of sand or something very like it. Isn't that a small fish, near the middle?'

There was certainly a slim object lying there, but the ends were the wrong shape and any movement was only the shimmer of the moving water. The tones, also, seemed wrong. 'I don't think so,' I said. 'If it is, either it's dead or it's picked an unusual lie.' As I looked, the object began to resolve itself into a familiar shape. 'I think somebody dropped something. Do you want to fetch it out?'

'Not particularly.'

'Then I'll go,' I said. It was warm in the sun and the midges were being drawn to our sweat. I was glad of the excuse to wade again. 'You keep watching and see what moves when I start wading.'

I descended to the river bank, entered the water and rolled up my sleeve.

'There was another salmon quite near where you waded in,' Eric said on my return. 'I saw it move and then it vanished. What did you find?'

I showed it to him. It was a hardwood rod with a leather thong and a staghorn end weighted with lead – a priest, the instrument for delivering the 'last rites' to a fish. Burned into the staghorn were the initials B.H.

'I hope that I'm there when you show it to Tony,' Eric said. 'I want to see his little face light up. Blast these midges!'

'You know what the entomology books call the midge?' I asked him.

'No. What?'

'The Scourge of Scotland.'

'They're right,' Eric said. 'Let's go.'

*

The coarse fisherman – by which is meant the seeker after coarse fish – may spend much of his day sitting on a stool, or in an armchair if he is so equipped, but the flyfisher spends the day on his feet, often up to his backside in cold water, stumbling over slippery rocks and sometimes fighting a stiff current. It was heaven to get back to the hotel for a leisurely bath and then to take a seat in the bar with no intention of getting up again ever, or at least until dinner was on the table. When Janet suggests that I am growing old I deny it vigorously, but the truth is that I am not quite as resilient as once I was.

I had left a message for Tony McIver on the police station's answering machine but there was no sign of him as yet. Harry Codlington was the only other customer in the bar. I nearly turned around when I saw him but I decided that nobody was going to spoil my repose.

As it happened, Harry was in a placatory mood. He insisted on buying me a drink and then took a seat at the table that I had chosen for myself. Even the space behind the bar was now empty, but he looked around carefully and then lowered his voice. 'I was out of order last night,' he said. 'I tackled that young policeman again and he said that my car's number was noted down by some busybody traffic warden. My apologies. Put it down to a dislike of being snooped on.'

'The feeling's universal,' I said. 'I quite understand.'

'That's good. I don't even know why I got so hot under the collar about it. As I think I told you, I went through for some casting lessons. I can cast a salmon line without getting into trouble, but I do a lot of trout fishing at home and when I start casting with a team of nymphs it soon becomes a quick exercise in cat's-cradle. There's an instructor at Granton who can analyse my bad habits and get me back on the straight and narrow in an hour or two, so whenever I'm up this way I book a session with him.'

'Very wise,' I said. I was about to add some advice about putting the heaviest fly or nymph on point and the lightest on the top dropper when Harry went on.

'So, while I was there,' he said, 'I called in to visit my fishing pal. To see when he'd be able to join me.'

'That was before he had to fly out to the States, was it?' I asked.

My question was an idle one but it seemed to catch Harry flat-footed. 'Well,' he said. 'Yes. He was to have joined me already ... that day ... but he had a problem and he'd phoned to say that he had to fly out and he didn't know how long it would take.' Harry paused. 'He was waiting for confirmation of the booking of his flight out to America.'

If Harry's friend didn't know how long he was going to be in the States, there seemed to be little point in visiting him to ask that very question, which may have been why Harry was looking as though he would have liked to call the words back. Rather than lay myself open to further accusations of snooping I said, 'I hope he'd already coughed up his share of the cost.'

Harry relaxed slightly. 'Oh yes. No problem there,' he said.

Tony McIver turned up just then and Harry, who was still in his fishing togs, made his escape almost immediately, crossing at the door with Eric. I transacted business at long range with Sam Bruce, who had reappeared behind the bar, and Tony obligingly conveyed the money to him and brought back the drinks before settling down with us. I might be Eric's guest but I felt obliged to stand my hand now and again.

'I don't know what Harry Codlington told you,' I said to Tony, 'but he's been contradicting himself to me. He tried to tell me that he went to visit his fishing friend in Granton to find out when he'd be able to join him and almost in the same breath he said that his friend had already told him that he didn't know how long it would take.'

'Is that what you wanted to tell me so urgently?' Tony asked.

I was nearly side-tracked into producing our treasure

trove. Eric was quicker to spot a diversionary tactic. 'We can probe a little further if you like,' he said. 'See what explanation Harry can produce . . . '

Tony flinched. 'I'll make any necessary inquiries,' he said.

'He'd wonder how you came to know about a conversation between himself and Wallace,' Eric said. 'We wouldn't want that. Wal can open up the subject much more naturally. You know the kind of thing. "I must have misunderstood you, because I thought you said . . . " What do you think?'

'I think,' Tony said, 'that you should learn to take a hint and drop the subject.'

'Ah,' Eric said.

I must have been slower witted. 'I don't follow,' I said.

'That just shows that you've led a pure and innocent life,' Eric said. 'What Tony daren't say aloud without breaching confidentiality is that Harry's friend had already flown out to the States but that Harry visited that address anyway and paid court to the grass widow. Is that where his car was improperly parked?'

'You would not expect me to tell you that. Now,' Tony said, 'what is it that you want to show me?'

'I was right, then,' Eric said.

I glanced at the bar, but Sam had vacated his post. I pulled out the priest, unwrapped it from my handkerchief and laid it on the table.

Tony set down his pint with a thump. Fortunately, he had already lowered the level. 'You've handled it,' he said indignantly.

'So much for his little face lighting up,' I told Eric. 'It had been under running water for nearly a week, probably rolling around on sand,' I pointed out. 'If you think you could find fingerprints or bloodstains on it, you're living in a dream world.'

'Maybe so. But I can just imagine a forensic specialist telling a court that he could only find snot and pocket-fluff on it. B.H.,' Tony added. 'Bernard Hollister, beyond what a court would consider reasonable doubt.' After a moment of hesitation he picked up the priest and weighed it in his hand. 'The heaviest one I've ever come across. This could dent a skull all right.'

'That's what it's for,' Eric said.

'A man's skull. I'll have to send or take it to Granton to be matched to the wound. Where did you find it?'

'About thirty yards downstream of this end of the bridge,' I said, 'on a patch of sand near the bank.'

Tony looked thoughtful. 'It could have been planted. Why wouldn't the searchers have seen it?'

'The water was higher then,' I said, 'and coloured and running faster, and there was a breeze. Today, we only spotted it because I was getting Eric to use his Polaroids and practise looking at what's under the water.'

'Even then, I mistook it for a small fish,' Eric said.

'That would account for it.' Tony sat, idly slapping the priest into the palm of his other hand. 'My day wasn't entirely wasted,' he said. 'I found one useful witness. The district nurse was called out late on Monday night to an epileptic patient between here and Imad Vahhaji's house. As she arrived, she saw him hurrying in this direction on foot. It was dark by then, but she'd be prepared to swear to his identity.'

'Things don't look too bright for Vahhaji,' Eric said.

'No. She also says that she saw a motor-caravan very like Hollister's. This was later, when she was leaving. She can't be certain, but she thinks that it came out of the hotel car-park. She walked out into an empty street, got into her car and when she looked again, seconds later, the other vehicle was coming towards her.'

The normal hour for opening had arrived. A group of thirsty locals came in and Alec made an appearance behind the bar. Tony slipped the priest into an inside pocket where it made an unsightly bulge in his jacket. Bea joined us soon afterwards, looking smart but very feminine in something blue – a cocktail dress, I think

Janet would have called it. While Tony was fetching her a sherry, more evening drinkers trickled in.

We settled down. 'Did you get anything from the girl?' Tony asked Bea.

She gave a small frown of warning. Rumours must have been circulating, because I was aware of hidden glances, and I thought that it might not be long before the Press got wind of a possible story.

'We could go through for an early dinner,' Eric suggested. 'You'll join us, Mr McIver?'

'Do call me Tony. Thank you.'

'But Jean will be waiting at table,' Bea pointed out. 'The small coffee room's probably empty.'

Tony went to see and reported that the room was vacant. We moved through, Eric pausing *en route* to collect another round of drinks.

'This is where I spoke to Jean,' Bea said when we were seated. 'I ordered coffee for two and then browbeat her into joining me. It seemed the simplest way to get hold of her.

'I didn't want her to get off on the wrong foot by lying or running to her dad, so I plunged straight in. I told her that she was doing Imad far more harm than good with her lies and evasions . . . if he was innocent, I said rather pointedly. That got her talking. Imad wouldn't hurt a soul, she said, he was a very gentle person and, besides, why would he want to hurt Mr Hollister? I pointed out that he'd had a dashed good try to strangle Mr Hollister and she said that it was all Mr Hollister's fault for saying something awful, she didn't know what, that Imad had been ashamed of it afterwards and that Mr Hollister had apologized. I asked whether she had heard the apology. She admitted that she hadn't, but she insisted that Imad wouldn't lie to her. I'm afraid she's not very bright.'

'But—' Tony began.

'I'm coming to but,' Bea said firmly. 'I said that that was all very well, but Imad would have to explain how he had known that Mr Hollister was dead and why he

100

had stopped showing his face before the body had even been identified. At that point she turned red and then white and some perfectly genuine tears came. She showed all the signs of somebody caught between Scylla and Charybdis.'

'Between who?' Tony demanded.

'Between two deadly dangers. She wouldn't volunteer any more after that, so I resorted to leading questions. Was somebody threatening her? Or Imad? Eventually, she gave in and nodded. Who? She didn't know. Had she had a letter? No. A phone-call? She nodded.' Bea sighed in exasperation. 'It was like an exercise in archaeology, digging out a little bit at a time and trying to fit it together, but in the end I got what I believe to be the truth.

'Very late on Monday night, she had a phone-call. A voice told her that Mr Hollister was dead and that there was a great deal of evidence against Imad which would all come out unless he did as he was told, which was to lie low and say nothing. Otherwise he'd be deported and sent home to his family in disgrace and she'd never see him again. There was more – veiled threats of violence but, from what little I could get out of her, nothing very specific. Or else she was too shaken to take it in.'

'The house that Vahhaji's renting has a phone,' Tony said. 'I saw it. So why would they route the message through the hotel?'

'I asked Jean the same question,' Bea said. 'She had never thought to wonder about it. But she also says that when she tried to phone Imad she couldn't get an answer. My own feeling is that they phoned her because she could be expected to panic and put more pressure on Imad than an unidentified voice on the phone. Or else that Mr Vahhaji would have been more likely to recognize that voice.'

'Any accent?' Tony asked.

'Not that she noticed, but she was in too much a dither to notice anything short of a cleft palate.

'She wasted some time dithering and then dashed along

the street, hammered on the door and poured out the story to him. It was after one in the morning by then and he'd already gone to bed with the telephone noisemaker switched off, but the first thing he thought of doing was to throw on some clothes and rush down to Mr Hollister's caravan to see if it wasn't all a hoax or a bad dream. But he returned to say that the caravan had gone and he'd nearly had a heart attack when a policeman stopped him.'

'Somebody stopped him?'

'Yes. That was because of the poaching incident, of course.'

'Nobody told me,' Tony said indignantly. 'Sometimes I wish that I had enough seniority to stamp heavily on fools. Then I remember that I'd have to take responsibility for them and I'm glad that I'm only a constable. Go on.'

'Jean and Imad talked it over and decided not to take any chances but to do as the voice had said. I think that's all that she had to say . . . except for one thing. She may only have been trying to divert attention away from Imad, but she insisted that, just around the time the bar was to close, she had gone out for a breath of air and found Mr Hollister waiting outside. He asked her whether Alec had gone home yet and she pointed out Alec's car, still in the car-park.'

Bea's quiet authoritative voice halted and she sampled her sherry while she awaited reactions.

'And there could have been a reconciliation or a major punch-up,' Tony said. 'I shall speak to Alec.'

'You'll have to wait until Monday,' Bea said. 'Alec leaves early on alternate Saturdays so that he can get the weekend at home. He belongs in Fife but he stays with an aunt near here during the week so that he can attend Aberdeen University in term-time and work in the hotel during vacations.'

'On Monday, he can explain why he did not tell me. So,' Tony said, 'by the time that Vahhaji walked down and over the bridge, the poachers had been and gone – possibly, just possibly, taking the body and the motor-caravan with them. Unless one of them was a local, I don't see them either knowing enough or thinking it necessary to stampede Vahhaji into hiding. I need time to think this over. Either those two have cooked up a not very probable tale or somebody bluffed them into a rather more convincing portrayal of guilty parties.'

'The bluff,' said Bea firmly. 'I don't think that Jean Bruce is a clever enough liar.'

'Far be it from me to contradict a lady,' said Eric, 'but I disagree.' He had been drinking doubles and was becoming flushed and slightly glassy-eyed. He was always inclined to become grandiloquent in his cups. 'The slightly dimwitted can make the best of liars. See how well it fits together. Hollister goes to Vahhaji's home, not to apologize but to continue the quarrel.'

'What quarrel?' I asked.

'That will doubtless come to light. There undoubtedly was a quarrel. Whether there was an apology or subsequent further outbreaks of violence, we shall have to see. Hollister returns to the river. It is getting late but the best fishing often comes as the light fails, true or false?'

'True,' I said.

'Vahhaji follows him. They fight again. Hollister gets hooked in the face and then zonked with his own priest. Vahhaji hides the body – perhaps under the bridge where it would go unnoticed in the fading light – and returns home, observed only by the district nurse.'

'What for?' Tony asked keenly.

'To wait for full darkness. And,' Eric said triumphantly, 'for dry clothes. Remember, he's almost certainly been in the river. Your house-to-house inquiries should be aimed at finding anyone who saw him heading for home, wet at least to the knees. He is thinking furiously. If the body is found here, his first fight with Hollister will be remembered. But a man with a motor-caravan is essentially transient. If Hollister is found in circumstances which suggest that he died a long way away, the fight may never come to light. When it's good and dark he returns to the scene, takes the dead man's keys and fetches the caravan. The path beyond the bridge is wide enough to take it.'

Bea nodded. 'Almost all that you've said would apply equally to Alec,' she said. 'But if either of them loaded the body at the other end of the bridge, what was the caravan doing at the hotel?'

Eric was in full spate. 'That's what puts Imad Vahhaji in the firing line. He called here to make contact with his lady-love. He could drive the caravan over to the Spey, but he had to come back again. It's a long journey by train and bus and he'd be leaving witnesses all along the way. So she would have to follow him in another car—'

'The white Mini that Mr Bruce gave her for her birthday,' Bea said. 'Not that I believe—'

'—and bring him back.'

'—for a moment—' said Bea, but she was not to be allowed to finish the sentence. The debate was becoming an argument.

'Or,' Tony said, 'Hollister burst in on him, brandishing the priest, and got dunted on the head right there in Vahhaji's house. When the officer stopped him – which has still to be confirmed – he had just thrown the priest into the river and was on his way to collect the motor-caravan—'

'Which,' Eric said, 'had already vanished, according to the ghillie and—'

There was a perfunctory knock. Ibrahim Imberesh closed the door behind him and stood calmly surveying us, very much his own man. 'His Excellency directs me to give you some information which has just come to our attention,' he said to Tony.

'I came here two weeks ago, to ensure that all was safe for His Excellency's arrival.

'Yesterday, one of the embassy employees who was returning home at the end of his tour handed over his notes and diaries to a colleague. From the notes it seemed that I had telephoned the embassy to ask for an investigation of a certain Mr Hollister. But the colleague noticed that the resulting information was to be phoned to a Bantullich number which was not that of His Excellency's house. So he thought to contact me and I confirmed that I had made no such request for information. I have that telephone number here' – he handed a slip of paper to Tony – 'and I believe it to be the number of the house where a Mr Vahhaji lives. My voice and accent would be easy for any Arabic-speaker to imitate.'

'And what information was furnished?' Tony asked.

Imberesh shrugged, managing simultaneously to express ignorance, apology and unconcern. 'Sadly, there is no note of this and we no longer have any contact with the man. But the request was for information about Mr Hollister's years working around the eastern Mediterranean.'

Tony frowned. 'Were you aware that Mr Hollister is dead?'

'You amaze me,' Imberesh said, without any sign of interest. 'We noticed, of course, that there was some unusual activity, but we do not have much contact with the locals.'

'The request referred to Mr Hollister by that name?' Bea asked.

If Imberesh was surprised to receive a question from somebody with no status in the inquiry, and a woman, his present veneer of polite unconcern prevented him from expressing it. 'It did. Presumably he had been recognized.'

'I shall call and take statements from His Excellency and his household,' Tony said.

'I will ask His Excellency but I do not think that he will wish it. However, I have here a signed statement although it adds very little to what I have already told you.' Imberesh handed over a slim white envelope, sketched the faintest of bows to the company and prepared to make his exit.

'Wait,' Tony said. Imberesh paused with eyebrows raised, the picture of a diplomat being hounded by foreign inferiors. 'You mentioned unusual activity. Did anyone at the ambassador's residence witness any activity near the bridge on Monday evening?' Tony asked him.

Imberesh shrugged. 'We are unable to help you. His Excellency had received a video of the news from home and we all watched it together. I am so sorry.' The door closed behind him while Tony was embarking on another question. I had the impression that Imberesh had delivered exactly as much information as he was prepared to divulge and that any further questions would have encountered a polite stone wall.

Tony sighed ostentatiously. 'There goes my chance of a decent meal,' he said. 'My landlady has no imagination beyond mince, neips and tatties. But I'll have to go and confront Vahhaji again.'

'What's the rush?' said Eric. 'You're holding his passport. He isn't going anywhere.' He frowned at the closed door, presumably aiming in the direction of Imberesh's vanished back. 'I wonder why that slippery Bedouin came with that information. He knew of Hollister's death all right—'

'Of course he did,' Tony said.

'Then why pretend not to know?'

'Just to be obstructive and to muddy the waters,' Tony said. 'The whole statement may have been made out of spite, because of the enmity between their two countries. Or maybe not. I shan't be sorry when somebody more senior comes to take up the white man's burden. Understanding the mind of the Arab is not for underlings like me.'

'Forget it for now,' Eric said, getting up. 'Come and eat.'

Duty and hunger were engaged in a tug of war. 'Perhaps if they could manage one main course in a hurry . . . ' Tony said weakly.

But he was young and hungry. With Eric's example before him, he made a good meal. When we were ready to leave the table, he looked at his watch. 'It's late,' he said, 'and I have reports to type and fax. You're right. Vahhaji can wait until morning.'

In the hall, he thanked Eric politely for the meal and said his good-nights.

I knew that a large parcel had come off the bus for Eric. My mild curiosity was satisfied when Eric collected it from the reception desk and pushed it into Bea's arms. 'Just a present,' he mumbled.

It was a moment for privacy so I said good-night to Bea and turned to the stairs. Eric reached the landing on my heels, puffing slightly from the climb. 'It was your generosity that put it into my mind,' he said. 'That and the fact that I hate to see her looking so dowdy. She's an attractive woman, don't you think?' he asked anxiously.

'Very attractive,' I said. 'And intelligent with it.'

'That's what I thought,' Eric said. He collected a coat and went downstairs again.

I decided that it was too early for bed. Archie Struan, I remembered, had always stayed up half the night. I left the hotel and went in search of my old friend.

On his retirement, Archie had moved in with his married daughter in a small terrace house which, I found, was only forty or fifty yards from the hotel but on the other side of the village street. I picked it out from among others of identical design. An uncurtained dormer window upstairs glowed with light in the gathering dusk.

I had felt certain that Archie would not go short of a salmon or two. After careful thought I had decided that whisky would also be inappropriate. His only other weakness, I recalled, had been for venison, and Sam Bruce had been able to supply me with a small parcel which I placed in the hands of the daughter, a comfortable woman in middle age with a roguish smile much younger than her years. She led me up a narrow stair and opened a door.

'Dad,' she said, 'Mr James is here.'

'I ken that fine,' said a well-remembered voice. 'I've watched him a' the way from the hotel.'

'He's brought you a puckle venison for our tea the morn.'

The old man smiled a greeting. 'You've not forgotten, then.' The room was a bedroom, but although he was in slippers and a warm dressing-gown over striped pyjamas he was established in an old but well-padded fireside chair in the dormer window. The curtains were wide open and could rarely have been closed, because a whole range of personal possessions ranked along the window-sill would have had to be moved. Conspicuous among them were an unlabelled bottle of amber liquid, several clean glasses and a small jug of water.

His hand gestured towards the other chair and then went out to the bottle. 'You'll take a dram?' he asked. He poured without waiting for an answer. I was glad of the confirmation that I had been right not to bring whisky. The 'water of life' is so true to its name in the life of many older Scots that it is rare for a house to be without at least one bottle with another in reserve, even when other victuals may be in short supply. I have never managed to explain this to myself except by supposing that there is a hidden economy, dependent largely on supplies finding their way out of the back door of the nearest bottling plant.

When we were settled with a dram apiece, he asked after those of my friends that we had in common and gave me news of others. Then I had to tell him, fish by fish and almost cast by cast, about our visits to the rivers Spey and Dee and he treated me to a valuable lecture about what flies to use and where to cast them in the present conditions of weather and water. It was cosy and nostalgic but it was not quite like old times. For one thing, there was a wistfulness in his manner, now that he was no longer a part of the river's lifeblood. For another, he seemed to be waiting for a chance to introduce another topic. I thought that I could guess what it was and decided to make it easy for him.

'And what's going on in the village these days?' I asked him.

He grinned with relief. 'It's been gey quiet until just a

week back. Then we had the poachers here and a right bonny rammy atween them and the bailiff and yon young laddie Gheen as took over from me.' He sighed. 'I'd ha' gi'en them laldie. Or maybe no'.' He looked at his fist, twisted as it was with arthritis. 'I think one reason they retired me was that I'm getting a wee bit old for the fechting. You heard about the poachers?'

'Bill Gheen and Ed Donaldson told me about it,' I said. 'It doesn't seem to have done the fishing much harm.'

'Likely not. I've noticed,' he said, 'a pool can be netted once and the lies are filled up again as quick as you like, but if it's poached again it'll not fish worth a damn for the rest of the season. But that's by the by. Then, just a day or two after the poachers, there was police a' o'er the place and searching the river bank. Then they was gone again and now, I'm telled, there's just the one policeman, no' long out o' the primary school, still asking questions and unsettling folk. There's none of the locals knows what's up, or if they know they're no' telling. I said to Jeannie that you'd ken what it was about for sure.' He filled my glass again and sat back, waiting.

The story was bound to do the rounds shortly, possibly in a highly garbled version. I guessed that it would do Tony's investigation little harm if the true background became public, while old Archie might have some useful facts to contribute. I gave him a brief account of the hard facts, leaving out all speculation although I had no doubt that the shrewd old chap would see as well as I did, or better, most of the implications.

'You'll keep this under your hat?' I said. 'At least as far as all the hearsay goes?'

'I'm no' a bletherbag,' he said. And I knew that he could hold his tongue when it suited him.

'Do you remember that night?' I asked him.

'The night the poachers was here? Aye, I mind it fine. Eddie Donaldson was at me to airt out if I'd seen their van go by.'

'And had you? Or were you in your bed?'

109

'I was up. I was never one for a long night's sleep, what wi' the late-night sea-trout fishing and watching for poachers. I'd make it up by snoozing at odd times. And now that I could sleep in if I wanted, the habit's too strong. And the rheumatics soon wake me again. I spend the most of my time in this chair, where I can see all that's going on, and if I feel like a sleep I maybe lie down on the bed or maybe doze where I am. It's a' the same. I told Eddie Donaldson that the poacher's van never came this way, not before near three in the morn which is when I fell to sleeping.'

It seemed important not to push him along too quickly. 'If they didn't come this way,' I said, 'which you wouldn't really expect them to do, you couldn't be expected to see them. Let's concentrate on what you might have seen, and if you've spotted anything important you can tell me whether you'd like the young bobby to come round here. Fair enough?'

He nodded gravely.

'We'll take it chronologically.' I tried to see past him, but without pushing him aside my view was limited. 'You can see the front of the hotel from here?'

He nodded again. 'I'm looking right at it. If it's Sunday night that interests you, I saw yon barman putting the twa o' them outside, yon dusky lad first and then the visiting fisher.'

'But the next night, the Monday, around closing time. Did you see the visiting fisherman, Mr Hollister, come back?'

'Aye. M'hm. The light was fading but it was still bright enough and I saw him fine. He spoke first to Jeannie Bruce and I saw her point to the car-park. And then . . . '

'Yes?'

'This is the way o't. From here, I can see the back door of the hotel and a bit of the car-park, but the most o't's hidden by the corner of the bakery. Ha'e a look and you'll see.' I craned past him and saw for myself.

'There's times he parks his wee yellow car where I can

110

see it, and times it's hidden away, it depends how the hotel guests have parked. That night, the car was out of sight. The mannie – Mr Hollister – had a while to wait before the back door opened and young Alec, the barman, came out. That was as much as I saw, but I can tell you something else a' the same. Yon barman, Alec, usually has a wee dog wi' him and leaves it in the car. Many a time I've seen him come out during his breaks and let the beastie out for a wee run.

'That night, it was a hot night and I had my window wide open. Just after yon Alec came out, I heard a noise. I couldn't swear on oath, but I'm a'most sure it was the screech of a dog. It was some while after that when the wee car drove off.'

'Did you see Mr Hollister leave?' I asked.

'No. But it was damn near dark by then and I wasn't looking in particular. Besides, Alec might have been giving him a lift in the car.'

That was an unpleasant possibility. I moved on quickly. 'What about later? Did you see the district nurse come by?'

'Aye. To Mary Callender's house. It'll have been to Mary's Jimmy, I'm thinking, the laddie that has the fits.'

'Did you see anybody walking around that time?'

'Not that I can mind. I heard footsteps, though. They turned down towards the brig and came back later, but that footpath's out of my sight.'

It seemed that I had struck gold on Tony's behalf. The information was coming in almost too fast. 'What about the motor-caravan?' I asked.

'Like a van wi' windows? Aye, there was one of those.'

'Did it come to the car-park earlier or later?'

'Than the footsteps? It came earlier and left again just after, about when Betty, the district nurse, went by. But it wasn't the car-park it came to. It went by and I heard it stop, but by then it was somewhere out of my sight.' He came to a halt and yawned hugely.

'I'm keeping you up,' I said.

111

'Damned if I couldn't be doing wi' a sleep just now,' he agreed. His eyes were closed already. 'See yourself out. But come and see me again afore you leave, you hear me?'

'I hear you,' I said. 'Good-night.'

NINE

On any fishing holiday the surfeit of fresh air, exercise and the occasional sniff of alcohol usually lull me into a sleep both longer and deeper than I can manage at home, what with Keith's eccentric approach to the pressures of business and a bedmate who radiates therm after therm of waste heat in the night.

But that night was different. I tossed, trying to find relaxation in a perfectly comfortable bed and to stop my mind from teasing incessantly at the questions surrounding the death of Bernard Hollister. The most obvious explanation, as expressed by Eric, depended on several weak links – inferences drawn from facts which, individually, could be explained more credibly in other ways. The next most promising theory, that Bernard Hollister had clashed with the poachers and paid the penalty, seemed barely credible within the time-scale. It was also possible that Hollister had waited for Alec the barman and that Alec, either bearing a grudge for a punch in the face or incensed by seeing Hollister kick his dog, had lashed out. None of those pictures satisfied the critic in me and in particular I had difficulty envisaging either Alec or Imad Vahhaji still angry to the point of violence twenty-four hours after the original fracas.

I slept in the end, but my mind must have been hard at work while I slept because I woke suddenly, to the early morning silence of a village on Sunday and a shaft of bright light through a chink in the curtains, with one overriding idea in my head.

113

My watch suggested that if Tony McIver was not already up and about he ought to be; and he had been rash enough to give us the number at his digs. My bedside phone could only reach the outside world via the reception desk, but I could hear stirrings below as the hotel came to life and after some jiggling with the instrument I managed to persuade Mrs Bruce to give me an outside line.

'Losh, man,' Tony said when his landlady brought him to the phone, 'I'm not long out of my bed.'

'I'm still in mine,' I said complacently.

'Then what can be so urgent that you have to have— ' his voice faded and returned as he looked over his shoulder '—that woman practically drag me off the pot?'

'Listen to me for ten seconds,' I said, 'and then you can make up your mind whether to get back into bed or not.'

'I was already up and dressed,' Tony protested. 'DCI Fergusson phoned me an hour ago. He may be coming through later, which will certainly make my day. Our inquiries about cars seen near Granton last Monday night are still bearing fruit. Would a yellow sports car surprise you? Make and registration unspecified.'

'Not particularly,' I told him. 'I think you should go down to the river here. Take a look under each end of the bridge among the weeds.'

'Why?'

'Because there's something missing. They've searched the banks, but I can imagine somebody, probably your sergeant, taking his men down to the bridge and saying "Search the banks from here downstream". That would be the logical thing to say, wouldn't it?'

'I suppose so.'

'Then what are the men going to do but what they'd just been told to do? They'd descend to the bank and start working their way downstream, leaving the bridge behind. The bridge is the logical place and it's the only place left.'

'For what?'

'If you find it, you'll know,' I told him. Now that I had

said my piece, sleep was coming over me in waves. 'This phone isn't very secure. And if somebody beats you to it, you'll never solve your case.'

I fumbled the phone back onto its cradle and slept for another hour.

When I made my way downstairs much later, bathed and shaved and dressed rather more respectably than for a day to be spent fishing, Eric was already at breakfast.

Jean Bruce came to take my order. Her eyes were puffy and I could only think of her manner as defensive. 'That Mr McIver was here looking for you,' she said. She sniffed, to show her disapproval of a policeman who played dirty by sending a forceful local lady to winkle out of her what she had managed to withhold from him. 'He seemed all het up about something. He's gone back to the police station to do some phoning, he said, but he'll be here later.'

'Was he carrying anything?' I asked.

'Not that I noticed.'

I ordered cereal, a boiled egg and coffee and she went away. Eric looked up from his mixed grill. 'What's going on?'

'Maybe nothing,' I said. 'No salmon fishing on the sabbath. It would hardly be worth my while going all the way home even if home wasn't filled with squalling brats. What do you fancy doing?'

'A pox on Sunday. It's the sort of day that gets God a bad name. I thought we might give young Tony a hand.'

'That's not my idea of a day of rest,' I said. 'I'll probably overhaul my tackle and go for a walk. I might even sneak a small rod down to where the burn comes out and try for a trout.' And without the distraction of Eric's company, I might have added.

I left Eric still working his way through a modest rack of toast and walked round to the shop for a brace of Sunday papers. The hotel bar was empty and cheerless so I made for the small coffee room. Eric joined me there almost immediately.

We were still deep in the newspapers when Tony

McIver poked his head round the door. 'You've had your breakfasts?' he asked.

'Yes,' we said together.

'A pity. I was looking forward to having a mid-morning snack with you.' He put a briefcase down on the table and vanished again, to return with a large cup of coffee. He chose the most comfortable of the vacant chairs, settled himself and stretched until his joints cracked. 'You were absolutely right,' he told me.

'That's good,' I said from behind my paper.

'But how did you know?'

I sighed and put down the scandal-sheet. 'I decided that we had to be looking at it upside-down. If the people we thought were lying were telling the truth, and those we thought might be telling the truth were lying, there was still one missing element. I told you my reasons for choosing that particular place to look.'

Jean Bruce came in and looked at Tony without affection. 'There's a lady asking for you. A Mrs Walton.'

'What does she want?'

'She didn't say. Shall I ask her to come through? It will give you somebody else to bully and badger.'

'He doesn't need anybody else while he has you,' Eric said. Miss Bruce gave a snort.

'Ask her to come through, please,' Tony said quickly. He sat in silence for a moment. 'Yes,' he said suddenly, 'I see what you mean. And I wish you'd given me that hint when you phoned me, before I spent half the morning typing up a report for Chief Superintendent Goth. He caught me on the phone earlier. He's coming out soon. He says that some fresh information has reached him.'

Eric put away his paper with a rattling noise. I saw that his eyes were beginning to pop. 'What the hell are you two talking about?' he demanded.

'Bernard Hollister's rifle,' said Tony. 'Carefully greased and put away in a glass-fibre case. Mr James phoned me early this morning and told me where to find it. Only, you were a little out,' he told me. 'I nearly missed it. It wasn't down in the weeds at all. There's a narrow gap that you'd hardly notice, between the concrete base of the footbridge and the railway sleepers that form the footway, leaving a broad ledge. It was pushed in there.'

'At the village end of the bridge?' I asked.

'Yes.'

'I thought it would be.'

'But why?'

Eric's question probably referred to why the rifle had been hidden, but Tony's mind had rushed ahead. 'We don't have the motive yet,' he said. 'But at least we know where to look.'

Eric goggled at him. 'I don't know what on God's earth you're talking about. And I don't believe that you do either.'

'Likely not,' said Tony.

Jean Bruce opened the door again. 'Mrs Walton,' she announced formally.

Mrs Walton came hesitantly into the room and we got to our feet. In an age in which women have abandoned their right to most of the old-fashioned courtesies in exchange for what they regard as equality, she was the sort of woman who still expected and got them. Bea might be just as much of a lady but she was also 'one of the boys' while Mrs Walton gave an impression of softness and femininity. Without being any great beauty she had a good figure, richly blond hair and a face which suggested a nature both gentle and loving even to the point of being passionate. She looked tired and her obviously good clothes were creased. They were lightweight clothes even for one of the better British summers and I wondered whether they had been chosen for their revelation of her figure. Her expensively styled hair was neatly groomed.

'Detective Constable McIver?' she asked, looking at me. Tony, apparently, was too young and Eric too overweight for consideration.

'I'm McIver,' Tony said. 'And you're Mrs Walton?'

Her face remained carefully blank, showing neither surprise nor disappointment. 'Helena Walton,' she said. When we showed no reaction, she went on. 'My father was Bernard Hollister.'

'Ah,' Tony said.

'Yes.' She glanced doubtfully at Eric and me.

'Mr James and Mr Bell,' Tony said. 'They found your father's body.'

'In the Spey?'

'Yes.'

Eric held a chair for her and she sank into it gracefully. 'I have been all over the place, looking for you,' she said plaintively. 'It's all very puzzling so you'll have to bear with me. My husband's at a conference in Milan and I went along for the ride, so to speak. That's where messages began to catch up with us. My sister-in-law phoned, the local police at Esher sent a cable and somebody came all the way from the embassy in Rome. They all said the same thing, that my father was believed to be dead and I was needed to identify the body.

'Jack couldn't get away, so I flew back alone and hired a car at Inverness. They seemed to know very little at Inverness and not much more at Granton on Spey, but I made a nuisance of myself and kept nagging away and eventually a sympathetic sergeant took me aside and whispered that you were the person to see.'

'You formally identified the body?' Tony asked.

'Yes.' She gave a ladylike shudder and her eyes filled with tears. 'That was Daddy. But I don't understand. What are we doing here?' She was younger than I had thought, as I realized as soon as I made allowances for grief and exhaustion.

Tony managed to superimpose an expression of sorrow for her loss over his relief that any remaining doubt about the identity of the dead man had been resolved at last.

'Perhaps we should leave you two alone,' I suggested. Eric glowered at me. Nothing was going to shift him.

'No, don't go,' Tony said. 'You've been more help than

anybody else so far. I'd like you to hear what Mrs Walton can tell me – if she doesn't mind? And you may be able to answer some of her questions.' I thought that he was more concerned not to be left alone with a woman who might burst into tears at any moment than over the lady's feelings or any possible comment that we could hope to make.

'I don't know enough to say whether I mind or not,' Mrs Walton said. 'Won't somebody tell me what's going on? Please?'

Out of her sight, Eric was nodding like an automaton.

'At first glance,' Tony said, 'your father's death seemed to be accidental. He might have fallen while fishing and hit his head on a rock. But there was some doubt as to whether he had died near where he was found.'

'You don't mean that he had drifted downstream. Do you? The fact that we're here ... '

'We think that he may have been moved.'

'But that suggests ... ' Mrs Walton's voice trailed away again. 'Do you suspect ... ?'

'There's a strong suggestion of foul play,' Tony said. Neither of them seemed willing to utter the word 'murder'.

'But that's awful!' she said. 'Terrible!'

She groped hurriedly in a doeskin handbag for a small handkerchief and dabbed at her eyes. We sat in embarrassment, as men will do. I wondered why it was worse to lose a loved one by murder rather than accident.

'I'm sorry,' she said at last. 'Please go on.' She blew her nose loudly. Her lace-bordered handkerchief had never been intended for such heavy duty. Eric gave her a handkerchief like a tablecloth. His manner suggested that he was close to patting her head or offering her a shoulder to cry on.

'We can't tell you the whole story,' Tony said. 'We don't know it yet. But events of the last few hours suggest that we're getting very close. I'll tell you all that I'm allowed to tell you as soon as I can, I promise, and, if I'm not allowed, Mr James might respond to a little coaxing; but Chief Superintendent Goth will be coming here soon and I want to be ready for him. We know very little about your father. Please tell us as much as you can about him.'

'Would it really help?' she asked. 'Because I can't believe that anybody would want to hurt him. He was a very mild person, very slow to anger.'

'And when he did get angry?'

She managed the beginning of a smile. 'That would be very unusual. At first, he'd be more inclined to wonder if he himself hadn't been at fault. An apology or a friendly gesture would disarm him completely.' (Tony met my eye and looked away again.) 'If he was in the wrong, he wouldn't be afraid to admit it. But once he'd decided that he was in the right, that was it. My mother said that it took him two days to get angry and ten years to forgive.'

'So it would not be out of character,' Tony said slowly, 'if, after a quarrel, he returned to renew it a day later?'

'A day later or a year later, either would be more in character than for him to pursue a quarrel at the time.'

'This is very helpful,' Tony said. 'Believe me. Please . . . '

He stopped as voices in the bar broke in on his flow. The door was thrown open roughly enough to bang against the nearest chair and DCI Fergusson made an ungraceful entrance. Jean Bruce could be seen hovering anxiously behind in the background. He slammed the door, blotting her out.

Tony McIver jumped to his feet.

'Sit down,' Fergusson said. 'I've come to take over.' He scowled at Eric and me. 'I might have guessed that you two would be here.' He looked enquiringly at Helena Walton.

'Mrs Walton is Mr Hollister's daughter,' Tony said. 'As it was Mr Bell and Mr James who found her father's body—'

'I understand that you identified him,' Fergusson said to her.

'Yes.'

120

'Perhaps we should leave you to it,' I suggested again. This time it was Mrs Walton who said, 'Please don't go.' It sounded like a sincere cry for support. I guessed that she had recognized Fergusson as a bully and that Tony's youth and rank were against him. Eric obviously had every intention of staying to lend her his support, so I sat back to await events.

Fergusson shrugged and dropped heavily into a chair that Tony had placed for him.

'You won't have seen the report I faxed this morning, sir,' Tony said.

Fergusson held out his hand and took the offered pages. 'You copied this to Aberdeen?'

'Yes, sir.'

'Carry on with whatever you were up to while I read this.' He began to flick over the pages.

'Please go on,' Tony said to Mrs Walton.

'But I don't know what to tell you,' she said, still plaintive. 'I don't know as much about him as I should. I loved him but we were never close, and now it's too late. When I was young, he seemed remote. I see now that he just didn't know how to speak to a young girl – a child and a middle-aged bank manager, we had no subject in common. And when I grew up neither of us could break down that barrier.'

'Try,' Tony said. 'Tell us what you do know.'

She looked reflectively up at the ceiling. 'He worked abroad for most of his working life, but I expect you knew that. Almost entirely in the Middle East, managing branches of the English bank. They did a lot of ordinary high-street banking, but latterly he seemed to act as a pipeline for money between London and the sheiks, caliphs and oil companies. Mummy always went with him. So did I, when I was young. It made life very difficult when I was sent back to school in Britain. Fluent Arabic isn't much use when you have to tackle your GCEs.'

'How did he get along with the Arabs?' Tony asked.

'Very well. Very well indeed, most of the time. He had

121

to be moved away from one of his first posts, he told me once, because he took the Arabs' side against the Israelis in any arguments. In Haifa, it was. After that, they were always in the Arab countries.'

I nearly interrupted, but Tony was up with me. 'You said "most of the time". Not always?'

'No, not always. About four years ago, Mummy was injured. It was a terrorist car-bomb, one faction going after another they decided later. It went off just outside their house. At first, it was thought that they might have been after Daddy, but it turned out that it had gone off prematurely and they were never quite sure what the target was to have been. The terrorists couldn't tell anybody anything, they were in bits.

'Mummy wrote to me that what upset him most was that the kitchen was flattened and if she'd been in it she would certainly have been killed. They were a very close couple. After that incident, he was unsettled. They might not have been so lucky, next time.'

Mrs Walton's voice and her story were so compelling that it was only when she paused that I saw that the door had opened again. The newest arrival was a man, as tall as Eric but so lean that Eric would have made three of him. He had grey hair, a saintly face spoiled by a nose which had once been broken and badly set, and mild eyes which I realized only later missed nothing. His summer suit was made to measure, contrasting with Tony's jacket and flannels and Fergusson's ill-fitting tweeds.

'McIver?' he said. 'Detective Chief Superintendent Goth.' He was so unlike his name that for a moment I disbelieved him.

Tony snapped to his feet. Chief inspectors might only have been sent to try him, but it seemed that detective chief superintendents ranked only a little lower than God and were much less approachable. 'I'm McIver,' he said. He managed to remember our names. 'Crucial witnesses,' he said. He introduced DCI Fergusson last. 'I was in the

122

process of getting a statement from Mrs Walton,' Tony added.

'I came through to take over,' Fergusson said.

'Not on my patch, you don't,' Goth said, quite amiably. 'Carry on, young man.'

Somebody, possibly myself, made a small sound of surprise and amusement. Fergusson flushed darkly.

'You explained that a near-miss from a terrorist bomb unsettled your parents,' Tony said. 'Please go on.'

'The bank was very sympathetic. Anyway, he was coming up to the retirement age for overseas staff. The bank gave him his pension and he brought Mummy home. They settled in Surrey and they were happy.' She dabbed her eyes again and blew her nose. 'I'm sorry, I'm being silly. They were happy. They had a large garden which they were developing together. And they both enjoyed fishing. Sometimes they'd do trips together in the motor-caravan, visiting the famous fishing rivers.

'And Daddy had some roe-stalking. When he went stalking, Mummy would go up to London for some shopping. Sometimes she came to visit me, but just as often she'd stay at the Overseas Club.

'That's where she was killed, in a stupid road accident and by a drunken driver, not many yards from the club. She had been to see a show with two old schoolfriends and she was crossing the street when she was knocked down by a car. She lived for another three days and Daddy was distraught. It was almost a relief to us all when she died.

'He went very quiet after that, became a bit of a recluse. We tried to bring him out of it. I made an effort to get closer to him at last and I honestly think that it helped him, but he refused all invitations and was cold towards his old friends when they went to see him. So when he rang up and said that he was going on a salmon-fishing trip to Deeside, we hoped that he was getting over it at last. He could have had years left and ... and people do manage to enjoy their lives when they're left alone.

Mummy would never have wanted him to be unhappy. She wouldn't have minded if he'd married again. She loved him too much to grudge him anything that would comfort him. Then this goes and happens.'

Her voice broke on the last word. We looked at each other and up at the ceiling, to give her time to recover. Eric was blinking furiously. The bar next door was open and the sound of conversation filtered into the room from a different world.

'And the driver?' Tony asked gently. 'Was he ever caught?'

She took a few more seconds to gather her wits and bring her voice under control. 'Oh yes,' she said bitterly. 'Although there was even doubt about that. They stopped. They had to, she was being dragged along under the car. The boss-man had been at a reception and he had champagne where his blood should have been, but they swore that his companion was driving – chauffeur or security man or something – although the club night-porter, who saw the whole thing, was sure that the boss came out of the driver's door. A whole lot of his compatriots turned up later, prepared to back up his story, but the porter said that the street looked empty when it happened. Not that it would have made much difference,' she added bitterly. 'They had diplomatic immunity, the pair of them. The Foreign Office sniffed around for a while, but they didn't want a diplomatic incident at what they said was rather a sensitive time and the whole thing was hushed up. Can you imagine that? They kill somebody, but because they're diplomatic they can't be touched! That, I think, hurt Daddy as much as anything – that justice couldn't or wouldn't even punish the culprit.'

We were so taken up with the impact of her story that the implications of what she was telling us dawned only slowly. Her voice, choking again, had come to a halt before I caught Eric's eye and then looked at Tony, to find that he was looking at me.

The question that had to be asked hung, almost audibly,

124

in the air, but before Tony could bring himself to ask it
DCI Fergusson dropped the report carelessly on a table.
'Very interesting,' he said. 'So the late Mr Hollister had
every reason to hate Arabs. He had a fight with an Arab.
He went to confront him again and ended belly-up in a
river, begging your pardon, Mrs Walton. I don't think that
we need look any further.'

'I think we should look a whole lot further,' Tony said.

'You *what*?'

'With all due respect, sir, I think—'

'Would everybody like coffee?' I asked hastily, getting
up.

'Very much,' said Goth. 'Thank you. And would you
ask the hotel if they can do me a late breakfast or a bar
snack? I was fetched out of my bed at three this morning
and I haven't eaten since.' Eric looked horrified at the
very idea of such privation.

As I escaped from the room, Fergusson was beginning
a lecture to Tony. Acting detective constables, I gathered,
were neither paid nor expected to think.

A few minutes later, when I returned, DCI Fergusson
was still winding himself up into a temper but seemed to
be running short of words. Eric and Mrs Walton looked
acutely embarrassed, the chief superintendent looked
amused and Tony, only half attending to his superior, had
written something in block capitals in his notebook and
shown it to Mrs Walton. She nodded.

'Breakfast had finished,' I said, 'but the bar is about to
open. They'll bring you a toasted sandwich whenever it's
ready.'

'Thank you. Next,' Goth said, 'I'd like to hear the rest
of what Mrs Walton has to say and I want McIver here
while she says it. But I want to test this Mr Vahhaji's
version of events.' He looked at Fergusson and then his
eyes moved on. 'Would you help me out by asking him
to join us?' He was looking at me.

'Of course.' It seemed for the moment that I was an
honorary member of the team. I took the slip of paper

with Vahhaji's phone number that Tony offered me and left the small room again.

The message was not one that I wanted to broadcast from the pay-phone in the hall. I asked Mrs Bruce for an outside line and went up to my room. Imad Vahhaji's phone rang and rang but it remained unanswered. If he had not taken flight he was either lying very low indeed or he was listening to his hi-fi through his headphones again. I went in search of Jean Bruce and found her laying the tables in the dining-room for Sunday lunch. When I asked her to relay the detective chief superintendent's message, her voice shot up an octave in panic.

'Calm down,' I said. 'Between ourselves, I think there's a good chance he'll get his passport back today. And you needn't pay too much heed to the threats. Any violence offered to him now would be counter-productive.'

'What?' As Bea had said, she was not very bright.

'Nobody has any reason to hurt him.'

'You're sure of that?'

'Positive,' I said, hoping to God that I was right.

'This isn't a trick? They're not going to arrest him?'

'If they were,' I pointed out, 'they'd have gone to his house, not invited him to meet them in the nearest pub.'

'It isn't a pub, it's a hotel.' She calmed down and began to remove her apron. 'Very well. I'll go and fetch him.'

'Tell him to wait in the bar until I call him,' I told her.

'In the bar?' I could hear panic back in her voice.

'Tell him that if anybody bothers him,' I said, 'he only has to move through into the small coffee room. Or just shout. One yell, and five large men will come to his rescue.'

She looked at me hesitantly, probably wondering if I counted myself among the large men and whether I was large enough, but in the end she went. Perhaps she was remembering that Eric was large enough for both of us.

126

TEN

I knew that somebody had visited the small coffee room during my second absence because the detective chief superintendent was eating a toasted cheese sandwich with every sign of enjoyment, watched in silence by the other four. The coffee was almost finished but I managed to extract most of a cupful from the pot.

Around Tony there was an air of suppressed jubilation. 'Mrs Walton confirms it,' he told me. 'The car that knocked her mother down belonged to His Excellency Abdolhossein Mohammed Flimah.'

'That doesn't change anything,' Fergusson said repressively. 'So Hollister had even more reason to hate Arabs. What he may have intended to do is neither here nor there. We have more chance of getting a conviction against Vahajji.'

Goth finished his sandwich and wiped his mouth and fingers with a white handkerchief. 'Not on the basis of what we've got so far,' Goth said.

'Let me interview him,' Fergusson persisted. 'I can get you the rest.'

Goth regarded the Detective Chief Inspector with increased dislike. 'Be careful what you say, Chief Inspector, especially in the presence of members of the public. Comments like that can be misinterpreted. A conviction at any price may look good in the statistics, but what we're after is, first, the truth; second, justice; third, a conviction. If in the process we come out smelling of roses, that's a bonus.'

The Detective Chief Superintendent's tone was mild and his words were no more than a gentle admonition, but I guessed that coming from an officer of considerable seniority they constituted a severe rebuke. Fergusson looked down at his fingernails in silence.

'Let's see where we've got to so far,' Goth said. 'I suspect, not quite far enough. Yet. Not that I'm decrying your work, McIver,' he added. 'Your fax was on my desk just before I left to come here. It's a good report. You've used your initiative to good effect, you give credit to others when it's due and when you haven't had the help that was due you don't bellyache or even make the point in writing. That's a good attitude. Any time you want to transfer to Grampian, I can find you a place in the CID. I mean it and I'll remember.' Tony flushed with pleasure.

Fergusson looked up sharply. 'Mr Goth,' he said. 'I'm on your patch so I've had to take what you've dished out, whether I agreed with it or not, but you're going too far if you think that you can try to tempt one of my best men away from me. Anyway, the boy's an idiot.' As soon as the words were out, Fergusson must have seen the conflict between his last two sentences. He turned brick-red and closed his mouth as tight as a trap.

Goth smiled but refrained from scoring the point. 'According to Mrs Walton,' he continued, 'her mother was injured by a terrorist bomb, which understandably put an end to her father's love affair with the Arab people. Then her mother was killed, and by another Arab. To add fuel to the flames of his wrath, it seems that she could have jumped clear except that she was still lame from the earlier injury. It seems very likely that the ambassador was driving but, whoever was at the wheel, it's enough that Mr Hollister believed that he knew who was responsible for Mrs Hollister's death – and that the culprit was avoiding justice by hiding behind his diplomatic immunity.

'So far so good. But all that we've shown is that Mr Hollister could well have had a chip on his shoulder where the Arab people were concerned which might have led him into conflict with one or more of them. We'll see this Mr Vahhaji soon, once I'm quite sure what I want to ask him, but at the moment I don't have the same hopes of him as a possible suspect as does Detective Chief Inspector Fergusson.

'First, let's consider the implications thrown up by the last item in McIver's report. The rifle.

'Let's suppose that Mr Hollister decided to take justice into his own hands. Mrs Walton, how does that square with your father's character?'

For what seemed a full minute, Mrs Walton sat with her head bowed. 'He was a very gentle man,' she said at last, quietly. 'Normally, he wouldn't have hurt a fly. But my mother's death destroyed the father I knew. He couldn't put it out of his mind. He was a different man; and that man, yes, given the time that would be needed for his anger to ferment he would have been capable of . . . what you're suggesting. Is it . . . only a suggestion? I understood that there was some question of salmon poachers.'

'I think not,' Goth said. 'I expect to hear shortly that the poachers have been accounted for.

'Very well, then. We can suppose that Mr Hollister found it difficult to get near his man in London. He had a rifle but no weapon that would be more easily concealed. The ambassador was in the habit of escaping up here and fishing the Dee whenever he could get away. It would not be difficult to find out when and where a man with such a public profile was planning to take a holiday, especially for Mr Hollister who was fluent in Arabic. The facts are that Mr Hollister booked the adjoining beat and arrived a week ahead, thinly disguising his identity with an assumed name. A further fact is that his rifle was found hidden, right at the boundary between the beats. Rather than have to carry it to and fro in full view, we can guess that Mr Hollister smuggled it into position by night and left it there, ready for use when opportunity arrived.

'Thus far, we have some facts which go towards proving

Mr Hollister's intentions. No more than that.

'By his own admission, Ibrahim Imberesh also arrived in advance of his employer, to check the security for the ambassador's visit. He seems to have been good at his job. He penetrated Mr Hollister's change of identity. It might be worth enquiring at the estate office as to how he managed it.' Tony made a note. 'We know that enquiries were made about Hollister by one of the Arab embassies. Somebody may know which.' Another note.

'Now we move from fact into what a court would regard as pure speculation. The ambassador arrives. He wants to start fishing – which, after all, is the reason for his visit. But he would never accept as coincidence that a man who has good reason to hold a grudge against him is in possession of the neighbouring beat. Coincidence or not, something has to be done about him. Mr Hollister comes and goes, but he is still fishing late in the evening, staying close to the bridge and waiting for his man to show himself. It seems that he had made no plans for his own escape. He was prepared to face the music if the ambassador was not.

'Imberesh and – what was the other man's name? – Bashari head for a confrontation with Mr Hollister. They may have intended no more than to disarm him and to warn him off. Or they may only have wanted to confirm his identity before reporting him to the police. We may never know. But Mr Hollister was in an excitable state. We may suppose that they came to blows and he was struck, fatally, perhaps with his own priest.

'Consternation. A full-scale diplomatic incident seems imminent. They carry the body into the ambassador's garden. They have been lucky, there are no witnesses. But if Mr Hollister is found near by, or if he disappears after having last been seen in their vicinity, the most rudimentary investigation would reveal the discrepancy of names, which in turn would uncover his grudge against the ambassador. But if he were found somewhere else, the death would have more chance of being accepted as a fishing accident. They decide to move the whole scene to the Spey.

'A reason that I am not inclined to credit Imad Vahhaji with the killing is that that theory leaves the ambassador's household up in the air, only involved by a remarkable coincidence. But if it happened as I have just suggested, we have an explanation for Vahhaji's involvement.

'Let's suppose that one of the ambassador's staff comes up with another idea for a fallback plan. There is a resident in the village who has had a violent quarrel with the deceased. He is a nervous man, easily intimidated. If he can be manoeuvred into behaving in a manner which could be interpreted as guilty then, even if attention focuses on the village here, any investigation would be unlikely to look further than him. They were reckoning without a persistent – and lucky – acting detective constable, but of course they always had diplomatic immunity to fall back on as a last resort. That, I take it, is how you were seeing it?'

'Exactly, sir,' said Tony.

'There is one more piece of evidence in favour of that solution,' I said. They all looked at me in surprise. I think that my presence had been forgotten. 'I visited an old friend last night,' I said. 'He lives near here on the other side of the village street. Being old and a poor sleeper, he sits up in his dormer window for much of every night. He was sitting up on the night in question and he saw only one camper or motor-caravan go by. He described it as a van with windows. It didn't turn into the hotel's car-park, which is in his view, but he heard it stop outside his field of vision. What he said suggested the driveway to the ambassador's house. I'll take you over and introduce you to him whenever you like.'

Tony McIver looked up from his notebook, nodded to me and then looked at the Detective Chief Superintendent. 'Sir, I'm puzzled by one thing ... '

'Yes?'

'Why would they go to so much trouble when they

were already covered by diplomatic immunity?'

Goth shrugged. 'Who knows how people will think during an emergency?'

'They killed my mother,' Mrs Walton said flatly. 'Now it seems that they have also killed my father. Are you about to tell me that they're going to get away with it again?'

'Not necessarily,' Goth said. 'Let's take it a step at a time. At the moment, we don't even have enough evidence to satisfy ourselves.'

'But even if you get a dozen eyewitnesses and a confession, they still have diplomatic immunity. That man who shot the policewoman in London was only sent home with a black mark, and he wasn't even an ambassador.'

'That is true,' said Goth.

Mrs Walton's face had a pinched expression. She looked less feminine and much less soft. 'As I understand it,' she said in a voice that shook, 'you have my father's possessions, here and in Granton. They will be mine now.'

Detective Chief Superintendent Goth produced what I think was intended as a fatherly smile although his broken nose rather spoiled the effect. He could have told her not to be a fool or he could have acted as a heavy-handed policeman would. But he decided to be gentle. 'When your father's estate has gone through probate, and if you are the legatee, and if by then you have obtained a Firearms Certificate, and if we are satisfied that you have good reason for ownership, we shall be happy to deliver the rifle to you,' he said.

As my ear became attuned to Goth's voice his accent of origin emerged from behind the veneer of education. In Scotland, and particularly the north-east, accents change every ten miles. His, I thought, had once been Aberdeen City rather than Aberdeenshire. There was a contrast there with Tony's sibilant Highland lilt or Fergusson's Central Belt growl.

'But that could take *months*,' Mrs Walton protested.

'Quite so. And by that time His Excellency will, I rather think, be out of the country.'

132

'And beyond justice.' Mrs Walton, her tears forgotten, was taut with fury. 'That's unacceptable. It's unconscionable. It just must not be.'

'Have patience,' Goth said. 'We may agree with your sentiments. But I am a servant of the law. This is the time for seeing what evidence can be uncovered. We'll worry about diplomatic immunity once we can be sure who's guilty.'

'There's one possible witness who's been overlooked,' I put in. They all looked at me again. I struggled on. 'You're short of evidence. There's only one avenue I can think of for positive evidence one way or the other and the man you want was in the bar, the last time I came through there. If you'll excuse me for a moment . . . '

'Bring him in here by all means,' Goth said.

I went through to the bar. Imad Vahhaji was sitting by himself, backed into a corner and clutching a large, amber drink as if for moral support. He caught my eye and looked a nervous question but I shook my head and made a sign which I hoped suggested both encouragement and patience.

Harry Codlington, looking slightly more cheerful than usual, was telling fishing stories to a small group of other disenfranchised anglers. When he arrived at what is called in television circles a 'natural break' I tapped him on the shoulder. 'Spare a minute?' I asked. 'Somebody wants some information. It's important.'

'What it is to be popular!' Harry said to his companions. 'I'll be back in a minute. Don't leave me out of the next round or I'll sue. Who wants me?'

'The police,' I said. 'They want you to help them with their inquiries.' Harry stopped dead. 'I put that badly,' I said. 'I haven't dropped you in it and they don't suspect you of anything. You may have seen something useful and that's all.'

I led him into the coffee room and performed introductions. With us, we brought Harry's drink and the rich smell of a bar in full flood. I saw Eric's nose twitch. 'Would anybody like a drink?' he enquired.

133

Goth smiled. 'I think we might stretch the rules for once. Why not?' he said. Eric made a long arm and stabbed the bell. Goth nodded to me.

'Harry told us that he was in Granton on Monday,' I said. 'This may be a waste of breath, but if he came back late enough—'

'Quite right,' Goth said. I pulled up another chair to the coffee table and we sat.

'We're still inquiring into the death of Bernard Hollister,' Goth said. 'You know what I'm talking about?' Harry nodded. 'I can't say more than that for the moment. Tell me about Granton on Spey.'

Harry's eyebrows went up. His mildly expansive mood seemed to have been short-lived but he decided to play along, picking his words. 'I went through for the day, to get some coaching from a fishing instructor and . . . ' He paused.

'We need not concern ourselves with the reason for your journey,' Goth said. I gathered that Tony's report had made mention of Harry's love-life. 'You went over the Lecht?'

'Of course I went over the Lecht. Why wouldn't I? Any other road that isn't about three times as far is very little better.'

Jean Bruce came in and tried to look questions at me while she took an order from Eric. Despite Mr Goth's assurance, Harry Codlington was ill at ease and refused the offer of another drink. Fergusson also decided to abstain. Goth asked for a large malt, Mrs Walton for a small brandy and the rest of us for beer.

'What time did you start back?' Goth asked.

'Late. It was dark. I was perfectly sober,' Harry said indignantly.

Goth hid a smile. 'I am not concerned with that, except in so far as it may have affected your memory. In fact, if you happened to have put a dent in a certain oncoming vehicle I might even be grateful.'

I saw Harry relax. He had, I decided, not only gone to

Granton in amorous pursuit of his friend's wife but had celebrated his success before driving back. 'I'm sorry,' Harry said, but more cheerfully. 'No dent. I can't help you there.'

'On the way back, what other vehicles did you meet?'

'Very few. You don't get a lot of late-night traffic over the hills. Most drivers try to time their journeys by daylight. When there's low cloud, it's like driving in thick fog and the headlamps throw beams of milk. On that sort of road, it's no joke.'

'How was it that night?'

'Clear. Some cloud in two places on the peaks.'

'What other traffic did you meet?' Goth asked again.

'I was paying more attention to staying on that truly awful road,' Harry said. 'I do remember . . . '

Jean Bruce interrupted us again to distribute drinks. Eric signed the chit. The detective chief superintendent added a single drop of water to his malt whisky and sampled it with satisfaction. 'Yes?' he said to Harry. 'You do remember . . . ?'

'This side of Tomintoul, I was going down one of those incredible one-in-five hills and hoping my brakes would hold, when I met something struggling up. I thought it was a van – I couldn't see much because he never dipped for me – but as I went by I saw that it was one of those caravanette things. And there was a car behind it, I remember, waiting for a chance to overtake.'

'And did he overtake?'

'I don't think so. I had a look in my mirror because, after I'd gone by, my lights picked up a wet stripe in the road as though one of them, presumably the caravanette, had been blowing steam, and I wondered if he'd make it to the top. The car was still behind. They were nearing the cloud line and the driver probably didn't want to face the risk of an oncoming car popping out of the fog all of a sudden.'

'What kind of car was it?'

Harry waved a hand in the exaggerated gesture of the

slightly drunk. 'I have the impression of something large and dark.'

Fergusson stirred. 'At what point in the journey did you meet the white Mini?'

Harry looked at him blankly. 'I don't remember any Minis, or anything white,' he said.

'Yellow?' Tony enquired. 'A yellow sports car?'

'Nothing yellow and no sports cars. In fact, I think the caravanette and the car following it were the only two vehicles I saw between turning off the main road near Granton and arriving back at Deeside. Apart from an old rattletrap of a van near Cock Bridge.'

'Thank you very much,' said Goth. 'That's all I wanted to know.'

'I'm afraid I haven't been much help.'

Goth raised his glass in what was almost a toast. 'You were more help than you know. On your way back, would you ask Mr Vahhaji to join us?'

'The thin, dark chap? All right.' Harry looked as though he would have liked to ask a few questions of his own, but after a momentary hesitation he turned and left the room. 'I think that we may be beginning to dot the i's and cross the t's,' Goth said. 'We'll get Mr Vahhaji out of the way.'

My time for a little dry fly fishing for trout was ebbing away. 'Perhaps we should leave you to it,' I suggested for the third time. Eric and Mrs Walton sat firm but I had just got to my feet when Imad Vahhaji sidled in, looking very neat and smart but more nervous than ever. He shot a terrified glance around the group, one known police officer and four strangers, and turned to me as the only person there who had sent him a message of comfort.

'Don't go,' he said. 'Please.'

Goth shrugged, so I sat down again. Vahhaji squatted on the very edge of the chair vacated by Codlington and laced his fingers together.

The Detective Chief Superintendent introduced himself and Fergusson, which did nothing for Vahhaji's peace of mind. Goth spoke to him gently. 'At the moment, evidence coming to us suggests that the statement which you gave to Mr McIver is true. But you must see that any lies and evasions can only count against you and make it more difficult for us to confirm what you've told us.'

Vahhaji looked at me. 'This is true?'

'Quite true,' I said. 'If you're guilty of anything, you should ask for a solicitor to be present. But if you're innocent, you can only save trouble for the police – and for yourself – by speaking up.'

As I spoke, I realized that my comment was double-edged. If Vahhaji now asked for a solicitor, it would be a confession of guilt – at least in the eyes of the police. It was a trap as old as justice itself. But he took it at face value. 'What do you wish to know?'

Goth led him first through what was no more than a repetition of what Bea had extracted from Jean Bruce. 'When you went out again, after Miss Bruce came to you,' Goth said, 'what did you see?'

'The caravan was gone,' Vahhaji said. 'A policeman came suddenly out of the shadows. I nearly ran away. Then I decided that I was trapped. He asked me what I was doing there. It seemed to me that all that had been said to Miss Bruce must be true. I said that I couldn't sleep and had come out for a walk. I showed him that I had pyjamas on under my jacket and trousers and he seemed satisfied. I nearly fainted from relief.'

'Did you notice anything else?'

'There were lights. But my distance vision is not good.'

'Lights, where?'

'At the ambassador's residence.'

Goth came at last to the missing element. 'Please understand,' he said, 'that we must know everything about Mr Hollister, his attitudes and anything that anyone might be holding against him. We can't accept your story in full if we don't know the reason for your attack on Mr Hollister. If it's irrelevant, it will be forgotten. But we must know.'

Vahhaji's hands were clasped together so tightly that I

could see whiteness spreading through the dusky skin. He glanced at me and I nodded encouragingly. 'If I tell you this,' he said, 'I must again open old wounds and say things which I had hoped to forget. But I will do it, not because I am afraid but because I wish to help you to find whoever did this terrible thing. It is true that I fought with Mr Hollister, but later I came to know that he was a good man despite what he had said.'

'Get on with it, man,' Fergusson said. Goth frowned him into silence.

'Take your time,' Goth said.

DCI Fergusson looked out of the window at the hotel's fecund garden and sighed.

Vahhaji took a few moments to settle down. 'Alec,' he said at last, 'the man serving at the bar, had told me of Mr Hollister's great loss and I was sad for him, because I am another who knows the desolation of the soul that comes when one loses a loved one. So when Mr Hollister asked for directions to the filling station which is always open, I sat down with him and told him how to find the place. He thanked me politely but his manner was stiff – I thought because of his pain. And, meaning no more than to help because my heart was sad for him, I told him of my own loss.

'I had a very dear sister, the baby of the family, and when our parents died I became as a father to her.' Vahhaji looked from one to the other of us. Tears were running down his cheeks but he managed to retain a slender dignity. 'We were very close. When she smiled the birds sang, or, if they did not, I sang for them. I wanted only her happiness. I hoped for a good marriage for her, but while I waited I allowed her to go to the university. There she became involved with a man and I thought that he might be the man for her.

'I did not know it at the time but he was a member of Islamic Jihad. He persuaded her to run away and join their ranks. I was frantic, but not all my efforts nor money nor family connections could find a trace of her. From

138

time to time, perhaps three or four times a year, a message would reach me. Usually it would be a short letter pushed through the door during the night with not even a stamp or a postmark to tell me where it was from. It would tell me that she was alive and well and that she still loved me and sometimes it would ask for the understanding that I could not give her. That would be all. I could not have answered her even if I had known what to say.

'The last news that I had of her was three years ago. I learned that she had died when a car bomb that she was driving through Jerusalem exploded prematurely. It was left to me to identify her, but all that they could offer me was the remains of a necklace that I had once given her. It was all that was left.

'All this I told him. I was about to tell him of my grief and then to explain that one can forget and go on living. An old hurt and a new happiness may exist together. Miss Bruce is helping me to know it and I hoped that I could help him.

'That is when he said what he did and for a moment I went mad.'

'What did he say?' Goth asked patiently.

Vahhaji suddenly folded down almost into a foetal position and his voice came muffled. 'Must I repeat it?'

'Write it down if you can't say the words aloud,' Goth said gently.

'No. I cannot run away from memory for ever.' Vahhaji sat up, squared his shoulders and wiped his eyes. 'Mr Hollister said that the explosion that killed my sister took place near the house he then lived in. He said that he found pieces of her flesh in the garden.'

Mrs Walton opened her mouth but Goth frowned her into silence. 'Go on,' he said.

'I can hardly bring myself to say it. We had never recovered any part of her body for sacred burial. I asked him what had become of . . . of those pieces. I hoped that he would tell me that they had been decently buried even if not in ground that I would consider to be sacred.'

139

Vahhaji's voice choked. 'He said that he gave them to his dog. To eat.'

The sounds of the drinkers trickled in from the bar but in the small coffee room the silence was absolute. The thought in my mind was that I had betrayed Vahhaji. We now had more than enough motive for a dozen murders. In his shoes, I would have killed if I could.

Mrs Walton broke the silence. As Imad Vahhaji's tears had dried, hers had broken. 'That was a terrible thing to say,' she said. 'But it wasn't true. Bernard Hollister was my father. He never lived in Jerusalem and he never had a dog in his life. He disliked dogs.'

Vahhaji slowly uncurled. 'So he told me when he came to see me. I did not know whether to believe him but I am glad to know that it was so. Your father visited me the next evening and apologized most graciously. He said that he had had a great fondness for the Arab peoples, but that his wife, your mother, had been injured by a terrorist bomb. He said that if her leg had not still been stiff, she would not have been caught by the car that hit her – a car that was driven by another Arab. This he was told by the one witness he could trust. So when I told him of my sister's work with Islamic Jehad and the accident which was so much like the one which had led ultimately to the death of your mother, his rage exploded and he sought only for words which would hurt as he had been hurt. Later, when he remembered exactly what I had told him, he realized that I had not supported the Jehad but had been a victim as he had.

'He was weeping as he told me, we were weeping together. I said that, although I could not forgive his words, I hoped that he would forgive the Arab peoples. We parted on good terms. If he had lived, I think that we might in time have become friends. We had much in common.'

Mr Goth waited in silence until the scratching of Tony McIver's pen came to a halt. 'Thank you,' he said, quite gently. 'Go home now. If you are in any doubt about your

140

safety, one of us will come with you. But I think that the threats made to you, through Miss Bruce, were intended to do no more than induce you to incriminate yourself, which you very nearly did.'

Imad Vahhaji got to his feet. 'I have been foolish,' he said. 'I will not trouble you further.'

'Don't. And go to your work by bus tomorrow. Leave your car keys with Mr McIver.'

'Do you want your passport back?' Tony asked him, accepting the keys of the Porsche. He put a hand on his briefcase.

'There is no hurry,' Vahhaji said. 'I shall not be leaving Britain for some months.' The door closed softly behind him.

'You didn't believe that load of bull, did you?' DCI Fergusson demanded.

Goth remained calm and polite. 'There are two levels of belief,' he said. 'Officially, I don't have to believe or disbelieve anything until all the evidence is in, and not even then. But unofficially and personally, yes, I believed him.'

'But think of the motive, man! All the talk of an apology was a clever blind.'

'Few men go through life without being given a dozen motives for murder. Thankfully not everybody acts on them. If Hollister had died that same night I might have been persuaded to agree with you.'

'Mrs Walton tells us that her father needed time to work himself up,' Fergusson persisted.

'Given time,' said Mrs Walton, 'he would have seen that he was in the wrong. He had struck the first blow, even if it was a verbal one.'

'So you're letting it go at that?' Fergusson asked Goth.

'For the moment,' Goth said.

'He should be in custody.'

'We have his passport.'

'Which you would have given back to him.' Realizing that he was making no impression on the Detective Chief

Superintendent, Fergusson heaved himself up by the arms of his chair and held out his hand towards Tony McIver. 'Give me the passport.'

Goth also held out his hand. 'I'll take it,' he said, 'for return to its holder.'

Tony hesitated for only a second. Goth was the senior officer and he was on his home territory. Tony placed the passport in Goth's hand.

'So that's how it goes,' Fergusson said grimly. 'I don't have to stay here to be thwarted at every turn. I'm going back now and I'll meet my procurator fiscal tomorrow. We'll see about starting proceedings. And you, young man,' he turned his glare on Tony, 'be in my office at nine a.m. on Monday.'

He slammed out of the room.

Goth glanced at his watch. 'Well now,' he said. 'We think that we know what happened, but proof, so far, is sadly lacking. It may be that the Forensic Science team can produce some evidence of the body having been transported in one vehicle or another.' He finished his whisky. 'I'm getting too old for being jerked out of my sleep in the small hours, but I'm beginning to revive. We'll take a break. I need to do some telephoning – and to grab an early lunch if the hotel is so obliging.'

'Use my room,' I said. 'Mrs Bruce will give you an outside line, if you ask her.'

'Thank you. Shall we meet again, here, at say two?'

'Does that include us?' Eric asked.

Goth considered. 'If you can spare the time,' he said. 'McIver seems to have leaned heavily on you already. It's a point in his favour. A good policeman should be able to enlist the public's help, not invite their active hindrance.'

'Sir,' said Tony, 'I think I know where we might get some evidence, but I could be wrong.'

'Go and find out,' Goth said.

'I may not be back at two.'

'If you're not,' Goth pointed out, 'you're not. And don't worry about DCI Fergusson. I can spike his guns for him.

Do you want to transfer to Grampian, and into Criminal Investigation?'

'Very much,' said Tony.

'I'll arrange to borrow you on secondment until we can fix a transfer. Run along now.'

ELEVEN

Bea walked to the hotel for a snack lunch and found me toying with a pint and a sandwich at a table in the bar. Despite the weekend, she seemed to have obtained the services of a hairdresser. I thought I could detect the faint complacency of a woman who knows that she is looking her best.

'Good afternoon,' she said. 'May I join you?'

'Of course,' I said. 'Shall I—?'

'Don't get up.' She put a friendly hand on my shoulder, pressing me back into my chair, and went to collect from the bar a half pint of shandy and one of the individual steak pies which were a speciality of the house. She sat down opposite me. 'Where is everybody?'

Among the babble of Sunday lunchtime drinkers we were as private as we would have been on a mountain top. 'Tony McIver's gone hunting for evidence,' I told her. 'Detective Chief Superintendent Goth arrived and is eating and telephoning upstairs. The dead man's daughter, a Mrs Walton, also turned up, exhausted by travelling, and she's taken a room and gone for a lie-down. We're to meet again around two.'

'I really meant Eric,' she said, 'as you very well know.'

I took note of the fact that she considered Eric to be 'everybody'. 'He went through to the dining-room for a proper lunch.'

'Gorging again?'

'He seems to have lost at least some of his appetite,' I told her. 'For all the breakfast he took, I could almost

144

have managed it.' I nearly added that he must be in love but I had the sense to hold my tongue.

She looked pleased. 'And the great mystery?'

'Seems to be nearing a solution but without proof.'

I expected a dozen questions about the investigation but she seemed to be satisfied to know that progress was being made. 'I wanted to talk to you about Eric,' she said. 'After all, you're his best friend.'

I must have let my surprise show. I liked Eric even if I was sometimes hard on him. It was a sad reflection on his lonely existence that I should be counted his best friend while he would barely have made it into my top ten. 'Well, that's the impression I get,' she said. 'He thinks a lot of you. And you don't say very much but you seem to notice a lot. I wanted to ask you something.'

'Ask me what?'

She took refuge in her meal while she gathered her thoughts. 'You remember the present he gave me?' she said at last. 'It was clothes. You probably guessed. I opened it up yesterday and went through it, even tried some of it on. It's beautiful stuff and well chosen even if some of the lingerie is a little young for one of my age. The rest of it suits and even fits me. It must have been very expensive.'

'Wholesale to Eric,' I said, 'and before tax.'

'That's not the point.' She hesitated and I thought that I detected a faint, becoming blush. 'I expect I'm old-fashioned. I was brought up to believe that a lady didn't let a gentleman put anything on her that she wouldn't let him take off her again. Gloves were acceptable, or a hat. Shoes only just.'

I kept a straight face. 'I don't suppose that Eric saw it quite like that. It just happens to be the line he's in.'

'He said that there were no strings. But there are always strings,' she said. 'He walked me home last night after you went to bed, and on the way he was hinting. No, not so much hinting as ... fishing. There's an apt word for you!' she said, smiling. 'He was fishing to know how I'd react if he suggested a closer relationship.'

I hoped that Eric had fished with more delicacy than he showed at the river. 'He's afraid of rejection.'

'You think so?'

'His wife didn't die on purpose, but deep down I think that he feels that she deserted him. Under all that flesh, he's very vulnerable,' I said.

'Don't be unkind,' she said severely. 'He only eats because he's unhappy. He misses Amy terribly. I think he sees the clothes thing as a sort of language, a way for me to give a sign without having to say it all aloud. But I really like him. I wouldn't want to get into anything I couldn't get out of – don't grin like the Cheshire cat, I'm talking about relationships, not clothes – anything I couldn't get out of without hurting him. Not unless I was sure.'

'I can't tell you whether you're sure.'

'No. But at least you can give me an opinion. Could Eric ever be happy with somebody else, after Amy?'

That was an enormous question. She had hardly touched her shandy. I fetched another pint for myself while I thought about it.

'Your voice throws him,' I said.

'Amy and I did sound alike. The family were always being confused, on the phone. Would it matter?'

'It would pass,' I said. 'It's your voice too and he'd soon come to accept it as such. His only reservation is that he thinks that you might starve him.'

'No fear of that,' she said, laughing. 'I enjoy my food too. I just don't like to see him overdoing it. I'd rather have a gourmet than a gourmand.' She became serious again. 'But if we had a relationship, if we married even, would I just be an Amy substitute?'

'Does any second wife start off other than as a substitute for the first? I think he's seeing you as a separate person already,' I said carefully. 'As I understand it, you look very different. He chose clothes to suit you, not Amy.'

'That's true,' she said, looking happier.

I hesitated before going on. Advice that seems good at the time can turn out to be disastrous. 'It's none of my business to advise you,' I said. 'I don't know whether either of you would be happy. But Eric's face, in repose, used to depress me, it looked so miserable. Since he met you, I've caught him smiling to himself. Looking at it from Eric's angle, he desperately needs somebody else in his life. He's free to please himself – but that's a difficult thing to do, to ask yourself "What do I want to do?" You might as well ask yourself "Am I happy?" or "Would I be happier if I did this or that?" The question is unanswerable or self-negating, because if you have to ask it you aren't. So he ends up doing nothing very much and hating it. One of the multinationals has been making offers for his string of shops, but he keeps putting them off. He could retire in comfort, but he can't visualize himself filling a whole lot of empty time. Not on his own.'

She had finished her pie and her shandy while this, for me, very long speech was in progress. 'The much-vaunted "pursuit of happiness" is a delusion?'

'Happiness is either there or it's not. You fall into it almost by accident. All you can pursue are favourable circumstances. But when you have somebody else to consider and to share with, the . . . the happiness boundaries are pushed further apart. Much further. Do you see what I mean?'

'Of course I do,' she said thoughtfully. 'What you've said applies as much to me as to Eric. I think . . . I think I'll go and try my new clothes on again.' She pushed back her hair with her fingertips.

On the phone the previous night, Janet had told me that her old friend had decided that a quiet Borders town bored her and had gathered up her brats and departed. Bearing in mind my hunch that the fishing was about to deteriorate, I found that I was eager to go home. But if I was too forthcoming I would lose the other half of my fee and Keith would boil over.

'Before you go,' I said, 'think about this. Eric still has

147

a week here. He doesn't need me – he takes instruction better from you. Why not invite him to stay with you? You could have a splendid week, fishing together. Who knows? He might decide that he could bear to retire here.'

'But what about you?'

'I could go home.'

'You wouldn't mind?'

'I should be happy to know that you two were having fun. Bless you, my children. Just don't let him know that it was my idea.'

We rose. Before she left she said, 'He did admire my house.'

I was back in the small coffee room before two o'clock. I had tidied away the debris from the morning's session and was making another attempt to read my paper. The first to join me was Helena Walton. She made a careful entrance, balancing a cup of coffee and a plate with another of those individual steak pies. I placed a chair for her.

'Did you sleep?' I asked.

She shook her head. There were dark smudges under her eyes and the flesh was puffy. 'I've gone past my sleep. And my mind's too agitated, wondering whether those men are going to get away with it all. I don't think that I'll be able to sleep again until it's over. What do you think is going to happen?'

'I could have made a guess,' I said, 'except that there's something else I wanted to tell the Chief Superintendent. Or Tony McIver. Or anybody else, for that matter. There just doesn't seem to have been a chance to get a word in. Try to relax and leave it to the police. Once they know what they're looking for, they usually find it.'

'And what then? Diplomatic immunity and a safe passage home?'

It seemed to be my day for handing out unsolicited advice. 'If that's the way it goes,' I said, 'then accept it. Mr Goth was trying, very gently, to warn you away from following in your father's footsteps. Do you have any family?'

She did not even blink at the apparent change of subject. 'A boy and a girl,' she said.

'Then your father had very much less to lose, at his time of life, than you do at yours. And even so, it cost him dear.'

'I suppose that's true,' she said, too readily. She fell to picking at her steak pie, crouching awkwardly over the low table. Something was going on in her mind. I had an uncomfortable suspicion that when her husband arrived back in Britain he would be invited to take up the sword, a one-man crusade against injustice with all the forces of law ranged against him. I only hoped that he would have the sense to tell her that the days of personal revenge were over, warming her bottom to emphasize the message – or else that he would hire a professional who would do the job properly.

The Detective Chief Superintendent and Eric came in together having met, apparently, in the bar. Goth was carrying a small whisky and Eric, to my surprise, brought with him only a half-empty glass of wine from his lunch.

Goth saw me glance at his drink and was not offended. 'My driver will come back for me when I call for him. No sign of young McIver?' he asked as he settled down, facing the three of us.

'Not yet,' I said.

'I hope that that means he's onto something. We won't wait for him. I shall have to get back to Aberdeen shortly, but first,' he said to Mrs Walton, 'I thought I'd bring you up to date. And you two gentlemen have been so deep in our confidence that you may as well know the rest, what there is of it. It may also help you to understand why there is a paramount need for confidentiality. Besides, you might be able to help. I would rather like to see this thing wrapped up by tonight.'

I began to feel rather sorry for the middle ranks. With Tony below striving to impress, and Goth above determined to make a point, they were in a nutcracker. And, if I was any judge, their nuts were going to get cracked. They might well report for duty on Monday morning to find that their chief and a very junior outsider had between them done what they should have done for themselves.

'Before you go any further,' I said, 'there's something else I should tell you. I didn't feel that I'd be doing you any favours if I'd produced it while Mr Fergusson was here to muddy the waters.'

'Go ahead,' Goth said.

'I'll try to give you my sources at the same time. Imad Vahhaji was certain that Alec, the barman, wasn't damaged in the original fracas, yet Alec's face definitely showed old bruising when we arrived here. Vahhaji also said that Mr Hollister went away to catch Alec in order to apologize, on the Monday night. Jean Bruce, the landlord's daughter, pointed out Alec's car to him. My friend in the house opposite tells me that Alec was in the habit of bringing a dog to work with him and leaving it in his car. He heard a dog yelp just after Alec came out of the hotel. Mrs Walton tells us that her father hated dogs.'

'From which,' said Goth, 'you conclude that Mr Hollister might have fallen out again with the barman over the dog, the previous night's argy-bargy flared up again and Mr Hollister ended up deceased?' He seemed amused but not displeased.

'I wasn't concluding anything,' I said weakly. 'That's your end of the stick. I just thought that you ought to know the facts.'

'Quite right,' Goth said kindly. 'All along the line. Right that it's my business to draw conclusions. Right to tell me. You would even have led me to a credible alternative theory but for some facts that I know and you don't, so you needn't feel bad about it.

'The business that got me out of my bed in the small hours was the arrest of the poachers – the same gang that assaulted the ghillie and the water bailiff here last week. They tried it on again below Banchory last night, but this time we were ready for them. Even so, it turned into a major scrap. They made a run for it and there was a fight when we managed to stop them. One of our cars was wrecked and two of my men ended up in hospital – the result of personal violence, not the car smash.

'However, we nailed the five of them in the act, with the van full of nets and salmon, and in view of the violence to police officers they'll go down this time and they know it. But their time after the poaching affray on Monday night is accounted for; they were stopped and cautioned for a faulty tail-lamp in Perth on their way back to base, all five men present.

'They also know the form and they weren't going to say a word. However, the fiscal's a wily man and he has a wide discretion as to whether, for instance, the two incidents are tried separately, or together, or the men are tried on one count and allowed to have the other taken into consideration or kept on file. These things can make a big difference at the time of sentencing, especially if the police are prepared to say that the accused had given help on another and bigger case.

'I don't know what sort of deal has been struck and, frankly, I'd prefer not to know. The latest word is that they've made statements about the Monday night and, of course, once one man starts to talk the rest can only follow on. They haven't taken us very far, but it's a start. They are ready to swear that Mr Hollister's motor-caravan was not in its place when they came past at around midnight. And when they reached the bridge there was an outside light on at the big house and two vehicles at the door. Then both vehicles drove off and the house became dark and quiet. The poachers set to work but the ghillie and the water bailiff arrived almost immediately.'

Eric sat up suddenly and snapped his fingers. 'And Alec the barman was one of them,' he said.

'Correct,' said Goth. 'Alec furnished the local knowledge. But there's not the least doubt that he was with them on the Monday night and that they all went on to commit another poaching offence downstream. None of them transported Mr Hollister to Granton, which makes it very unlikely that they offered him any violence.'

'And it's too much to hope that they recognized the motor-caravan outside the ambassador's house?' Eric asked.

'Unfortunately, yes,' said Goth. 'However, the rest of my news may be considered more promising. I have also spent some time on the phone to the Foreign Office. Sunday or not, the switchboard was manned and I was able to make contact with somebody conversant with the situation in the Middle East.

'At the time when Mrs Hollister died, it would have been impolitic to proceed against the ambassador. Since then, there has been a shift of power in his country, to a faction of which Her Majesty's Government disapproves. The new rulers would very much like to mend fences with the West, but our government is rather hoping for an excuse to show signs of its disapproval.'

'Would they agree to a prosecution?' Mrs Walton asked quickly.

'At first glance, diplomatic immunity would seem to hold good. But given some proof of a criminal offence – not necessarily sufficient proof to satisfy a court of law, but enough to make it clear to the world that the action was not taken lightly – they would be prepared to declare the ambassador and his household *personae non gratae*, or whatever the proper plural may be.'

'And they get off again,' Mrs Walton said.

'You could say so. On the other hand, the ambassador's family is not favoured by the new regime. They have been stripped of money and power and several of them seem to have disappeared. A return home in disgrace, after doing serious damage to relations which the regime had been trying to improve, would not exactly be greeted with a red carpet. They would be lucky to end up guarding the new emir's harem, after suitable surgical intervention.'

One tends to forget how primitive some parts of the world remain, even parts which, because of close trade associations, gain an illusion of familiarity. It took a few seconds for Goth's last few words to sink in. Then I felt a shiver up my back and I saw Eric flinch.

'I could settle for that,' Mrs Walton said grimly.

'At last we have an explanation of why they tried so hard to cover up the killing instead of relying on diplomatic immunity,' I said.

'Quite so,' Goth said. 'In fact, there had already been some tentative discussions about political asylum. Now consider this for a moment. Faced with the consequences of being sent home in disgrace the ambassor and his men might well prefer to take a chance on political asylum, even if a condition of it were to be that they forgo their diplomatic immunity, retrospectively, and take their chances in a British court.'

'I would rather see them sent home,' Mrs Walton said, 'if you are right.'

Goth nodded, keeping his face impassive. 'I expect you would. And it may come to that. Happily for them, the decision is not yours. So far, the case rests largely on motive, which has little value as evidence. Millions of people may have a motive for a bullion robbery, but they can't all be guilty. Now that we know who to ask and what to ask them, we may be able to build up a case and, of course, forensic science may come to our aid. But for the moment we are still far short of the necessary proof.' He looked past us. 'Or are we?'

'Perhaps not,' said Tony's voice. At some point while the Detective Chief Superintendent was speaking, he had come into the room and stood waiting. Now he came forward and slipped into the spare chair.

'This morning,' he said, 'when Imad Vahhaji mentioned the all-night filling station, at first I couldn't think why Mr James was making faces at me. Then it occurred to me. On Sunday, Mr Hollister was asking the way to it. So the motor-caravan was short of fuel. But a few minutes later he became rather preoccupied and he seems to have been fishing for all of the Monday until his death. If somebody wanted to drive the caravan to the Spey on

Monday night, they might have found it short of petrol and have had to fill up before going over the Lecht. Of course, they might have siphoned petrol out of another car, but it was worth a try.

'At best, I hoped that whoever was doing pump duty at the filling station today could give me the address of whoever was doing the same duty on Monday night. Then there was a faint chance that that person might remember the caravan and who was driving it.'

'And did he?' asked Mrs Walton.

Tony McIver held up a hand for patience. 'As it turns out, Sunday afternoon is the time when the proprietor comes in to do his accounts and VAT and so on. And he's the meticulous type who insists on vehicle numbers being entered on credit card slips, just in case the card had been stolen.

'Late on Monday night, or to be more precise very early on Tuesday morning, Ali Bashari filled up both Mr Hollister's motor-caravan and the ambassador's car. And – would you believe it? – he used the embassy credit card.'

'Wow!' said Eric.

Mrs Walton broke the ensuing silence with a protracted yawn. 'I'm going up to my room,' she said. 'I think I could sleep now.'

EPILOGUE

The ambassador and his staff accepted political asylum, giving up their diplomatic immunity.

Ibrahim Imbaresh and Ali Bashari pleaded guilty to manslaughter and this reduced plea was accepted.

His former Excellency Abdolhossein Mohammed Flimah was defended by a senior silk. His two associates might have ameliorated their own stiff sentences by implicating him but, perhaps out of fear, they did not. Without any direct evidence that he was associated with them in the death and transportation of Mr Hollister, he was acquitted.

The case had attracted the attention of the media. Mr Flimah was telling the Press and television cameras of his delight in having his innocence proved and reaffirming his faith in British justice when he was shot dead by means of a pistol hidden in the dummy camera of a supposed reporter. His killer escaped but was later identified, from the shots taken by genuine press photographers, as a professional assassin more often working in the Middle East. It was therefore assumed that the killing was politically inspired.

Only Mrs Walton could have confirmed or denied that assumption, and if anybody had thought to ask her it is unlikely that her answer could have been relied on.